Harlequin Romance™ is thrilled to present another
wonderful book from award-winning author

Liz Fielding

Liz will keep you captivated for hours with her
contemporary, witty and feel-good romances....

About *A Surprise Christmas Proposal:*

"Liz Fielding's newest is simply a gem. Sophie is
Bridget Jones without self-pity, and Gabriel's a hero
any woman would love to find in her stocking."
—*Romantic Times BOOKclub*

About *City Girl in Training:*

"One of the best Harlequin Romances this reviewer
has ever read. This story is exciting, fresh, innovative
and a breath of fresh air, yet it is told in the traditional
sweet tone of the line, which will make
this book appeal to all readers."
—*Romantic Times BOOKclub*

For a few minutes, he'd talked to her as if she was whole. Saying things that no one else would have dreamed of saying. Asking her if she tap-danced....

And even when he'd realized that tap dancing was not, never would be, part of her repertoire he hadn't changed, hadn't started talking to her as if she was witless. Dinner with him would have been a rare pleasure. Sitting together at a candlelit table, she could have pretended for a few dizzy hours that on the outside she was like any other woman. The way she was deep inside. With the same longings. The same desire to be loved, to have a man hold her, make love to her.

She closed her eyes for a moment, shutting out the reminders that she was not, would never be, like other women. Then, with a deep breath, she opened them again.

He'd been there, in her head since the moment he'd taken her hand, held it a touch too long. Been there the minute she'd stopped concentrating on something else.

In A Wife on Paper Francesca Lang's dreams came true when Guy Dymoke stole her heart. In this equally emotional story by award-winning author Liz Fielding, will Francesca's cousin Matty find the same success with the man of her dreams...?

THE MARRIAGE
MIRACLE

Liz Fielding

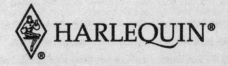

HARLEQUIN®

TORONTO • NEW YORK • LONDON
AMSTERDAM • PARIS • SYDNEY • HAMBURG
STOCKHOLM • ATHENS • TOKYO • MILAN • MADRID
PRAGUE • WARSAW • BUDAPEST • AUCKLAND

ISBN 0-373-03885-2

THE MARRIAGE MIRACLE

First North American Publication 2006.

Copyright © 2005 by Liz Fielding.

Liz Fielding started writing at the age of twelve, when she won a writing competition at school. After that early success there was quite a gap—during which she was busy working in Africa and the Middle East, getting married and having children—before her first book was published in 1992. Now readers worldwide fall in love with her irresistible heroes and adore her independent-minded heroines. Visit Liz's Web site for news and extracts of upcoming books at www.lizfielding.com

Books by Liz Fielding

HARLEQUIN ROMANCE®
3837—A WIFE ON PAPER
3853—HER WISH-LIST BRIDEGROOM
3872—A NANNY FOR KEEPS

CHAPTER ONE

FUNERALS and weddings. Sebastian Wolseley hated them both. At least the first had absolved him from attending the more tedious part of the second. And gave him a cast-iron excuse to leave the celebrations once he'd done his duty by one of his oldest friends.

The last thing he felt like doing was celebrating.

'You look as if you could do with something stronger.'

He turned from his depressed contemplation of the glass in his hand to acknowledge the woman who'd broken into his thoughts. She was the sole occupant of a table littered with the remains of the lavish buffet. The only one who had not decamped to the marquee and the dance floor. From the cool, steady way she was looking at him he had the unsettling notion that she'd been watching him, unnoticed, for some time. But then she wasn't the kind of woman you'd notice.

Her colouring was non-descript, mousy. She was too thin for anything approaching beauty, and her pick-up line was too corny to hook his interest. But her features were strong, her eyes glittered with intelligence and it was more than just good manners that stopped him from putting down the glass and walking away.

'Do you tap dance for an encore?' he asked.

She lifted her eyebrows, but she didn't smile. 'Tap dance?'

'You're not the cabaret? A mind-reading act, perhaps?' He heard the biting sarcasm coming from his mouth and wished he'd walked. He had no business inflicting his black mood on innocent bystanders. Or sitters.

'It doesn't take a mind-reader to see that you're not exactly focussed on this whole "til-death-us-do-part" thing,' she countered, still not smiling, but not storming off, offended, either. 'You've been holding your glass for so long that the contents must be warm. In fact, I'd go so far as to suggest that you'd look more at home at a wake than at a reception to celebrate the blessing of a marriage.'

'Definitely a mind-reader,' he said, finally abandoning the barely touched glass on her table. 'Although I have a feeling that the wake I've just left will by now be making this party look sedate.'

And then he felt really guilty.

First he'd been rude to the woman, and when that hadn't driven her away he'd tried to embarrass her. Apparently without success. She merely tilted her head slightly to the side, reminding him of an inquisitive bird.

'Was it someone close?' she enquired, rejecting the usual hushed, reverential tone more usually adopted when speaking to the recently bereaved. She might just as easily have been asking him if he'd like a cup of tea.

Such matter-of-factness was an oddly welcome respite from the madness that had overtaken his life in the last week and for the first time in days he felt a little of the tension slip away.

'Close enough. It was my mad, bad Uncle George.' Then, 'Well, he was a distant cousin, actually, but he was so much older...'

She propped her elbows on the table, framing her chin with her hands. 'In what way was he mad and bad?'

'In much the same way as his namesake, Byron.'

Even in the dusky twilight of a long summer evening, with only candles and the fairy lights strung from the trees for illumination, her face had no softness, nothing of conventional prettiness, but her fine skin was stretched over good bones. The strength, it occurred to him, came from within. She wasn't flirting with him. She was interested.

'Mad, bad and dangerous to know. Such a temptation for foolish women. So, was the riotous wake an expression of relief?' she continued earnestly. 'Or a celebration of a life lived to the full?'

Too late now to walk away, even if he'd wanted to, and, pulling out the chair opposite her, he sat down.

'That rather depends on your point of view. The family tended to the former, his friends to the latter.'

'And you?'

He sat back. 'I'm still struggling to come to terms with it,' he said. 'But how many people, knowing that they have weeks left, would take the trouble to arrange the kind of theatrical exit that would bring joy to their friends and scandalise their family? The kind of extravagant wake that people will be talking about for years?'

'Theatrical?' She looked thoughtful. 'Are we talking black horses? Ostrich plumes?'

'The works. Queen Victoria would have been proud,' he said. 'Although whether she would have been amused by a wake at which nothing but smoked salmon, caviar and vintage champagne is served, I'm not so sure.'

'Sounds good to me.'

'Yes, well, he wanted everyone to have a damn good time; an instruction which his many friends are, even now, taking to their hearts.'

'That doesn't sound mad or bad to me, but rather wonderful. So why aren't you?'

'Having a damn good time?' Good question. 'Perhaps because I'm in mourning for my own life.' She waited, apparently the perfect listener, recognising that he needed

someone to talk to, knowing that sometimes only a
stranger would do. 'I'm the one he nominated to clear up
the empties—metaphorically speaking—when the party-
ing is done.'

'Really?' She didn't miss the oddity that he'd choose
a much younger, apparently distant relative. 'You're a
lawyer?'

'A banker.'

'Oh, well, that's a good choice.'

'Not if you're the banker in question.'

She pulled a face. Not exactly a smile, but oddly cheer-
ing nonetheless. 'Obviously the reckoning is about more
than a few crates of champagne.'

'I'm afraid so. But you're right—it's terribly bad manners to bring my troubles to a wedding. I really hadn't
intended doing more than putting in an appearance to toast
the happy couple, and I've done that. I should call a taxi.'

He didn't move.

'Would a decent single-malt whisky help lay your
ghosts?'

There was nothing of the mouse about her eyes, he
decided. They were an unusual colour, more amber than
brown, with a fringe of thick lashes, and her mouth was
wide and full. He had a sudden notion to see it smile,
really smile.

'It might,' he conceded. 'I'm prepared to give it a try
if you'll join me.' Then he looked towards the heaving
marquee and wished he'd kept his mouth shut. The last
thing he wanted to do was push his way through the joyful
throng to the bar.

'No need to battle through the dancing hordes,' she
assured him. 'Just go through those French windows and
you'll find a decanter on the sofa table.'

He glanced towards the house, then at her, this time rather more closely.

'Making rather free with our host's hospitality, aren't you?' he suggested, vaguely surprised to discover that he was the one grinning.

'He wouldn't object. But in this instance the hospitality is mine. I live in the garden flat,' she said, offering her hand. 'Matty Lang. Best woman and cousin to the bride.'

'Sebastian Wolseley,' he replied, taking it. Her hand was small, but there was nothing soft about it and her grip was firm.

'The big-shot New York banker? I wondered what you'd look like when I was writing the invitations.'

'You did?' He recalled the exquisite copperplate script that had adorned the gilt-edged invitation card to the blessing of the marriage of Francesca and Guy Dymoke and the reception they were holding in their garden to celebrate the fact. 'Isn't it the bride's job to write the invitations?'

'I've no idea, but in the event the bride had other things on her mind at the time.'

'Oh, well, so long as she has time to concentrate on her marriage I don't suppose it matters who writes them. She runs her own company, I understand.'

'She didn't have much choice,' Matty replied, rather less cordially, and it occurred to him that he must have sounded unnecessarily critical.

'No?' he asked, not especially interested in who'd written the invitations or why. But he'd been rude—wedding celebrations tended to bring out the worst in him; good manners demanded that he allow his victim to put him right.

'No,' she repeated. 'But on this occasion she wasn't

upstairs, busily drumming up some brilliant new PR stunt, she was in the throes of childbirth.'

'That would certainly count as a legitimate excuse,' he agreed.

Perhaps deciding that she'd overreacted slightly, Matty Lang lifted her shoulders in a minimal shrug. 'To be honest, I did feel a bit guilty afterwards. She really wanted to write them herself. But I had to do something to keep my mind occupied and I'd have only been in the way upstairs.'

'You did them quite beautifully,' he assured her. 'I hope she was properly grateful.'

'Gratitude doesn't come into it.' Then, 'Are you and Guy close friends?' she asked, not that easily appeased. 'Or is this duty visit simply the gloss on a thoroughly bloody day?'

'I didn't say it was a duty visit. Merely that I hadn't intended to stay for long. As for friendship, well, Guy and I bonded at university over our mutual interest in beer and women...' Realising that was perhaps not the most tactful thing to say at the man's wedding celebrations, he took a verbal sidestep and went on, 'But you're right; we haven't seen nearly enough of one another in the last few years. I live...' *lived*, he mentally corrected himself, *lived* '...in New York. And Guy never stayed put in one place long enough for me to catch up with him.'

'He's a regular stay-at-home these days, I promise you,' she assured him.

'Good for him.' Then, 'Why?'

'Why is he a regular stay-at-home?'

'One look at his wife answers that question,' he replied. 'Why did you want to know what I look like?'

'Oh, I see. Well, as best woman I get the pick of the unattached males.' At which point he was amused to see the faintest touch of a blush colour the cheeks of the very cool Miss Lang. 'Guy, I have to tell you, was no help,' she went on quickly. 'The best he could come up with for you was "tallish and darkish". Friends you might be, but my enquiry regarding the colour of your eyes met with a total blank.'

'No? Well, to be honest I couldn't say what colour his are, either, but it's been a while since we've been in the same country.'

'His excuse was that he'd left gazing into your eyes to the countless females who trailed after you. But even if he had been that observant, I can well understand his difficulty.'

'Okay, I'm hooked. In what way are my eyes difficult?'

'They're not difficult, just changeable. At first sight I would have said they were grey, but now I'm not so sure.' Then, 'Drink?' she prompted. 'Add a little water to mine. Not too much.'

'Are you sure you shouldn't be doing your best woman duty and strutting your stuff with the best man?'

There was just the tiniest hesitation before she said, 'Would you believe he's married? To the most gorgeous redhead you've ever seen. I ask you, what's the point of a best man who isn't available for the best woman to have her wicked way with? I can't believe someone as smart as Guy could get it so wrong.'

'Shocking,' he said, almost but not totally certain that she was kidding. Women usually smiled at him. This one didn't. He'd changed his mind about her flirting, she *was* flirting, quite outrageously, but she didn't smile, or bat her eyelashes, or do anything that women usually did. He wasn't exactly sure what she was doing, but she'd got his full attention. 'Definitely time for that drink.' Then, since flirting under any circumstances should not be a one-way transaction, 'Unless I can offer myself as a substitute?'

'For the best man?'

'Since you've been so badly let down,' he confirmed.

Guy had asked him, but he hadn't anticipated being in London at the time...

'Are you suggesting that we disappear into the shrubbery and fool around, Mr Wolseley?'

Her gaze was steady as a rock, and that wide mouth hadn't so much as twitched. For a moment he found himself floundering, as if he'd stepped unexpectedly out of his depth.

He took a slow breath to steady himself and said, 'Well, to be honest, that's a little fast for me, Miss Lang. I like to get to know a girl before I take her clothes off. And I prefer to do it in comfort.'

'That's no fun. Not entering into the spirit of the thing at all.'

'I don't have to know her *that* well,' he said seriously. 'A dance or two—dinner, maybe? Once that hurdle is passed and we get to first-name terms I'm perfectly willing to be led astray.'

'But only in comfort.'

'I like to take my time.'

Without warning her face lit up in the kind of smile that took the sting out of his day, so that dancing with her seemed like the best idea he'd had for a long time.

'You like to dance?' she asked.

He had the oddest feeling that he was being tested in some way. 'Yes, but we can pass if you're hungry. Go straight to dinner.'

'And are you good?'

Definitely being tested.

'At dancing?'

'That's what we were talking about,' she reminded him.

'Was it?' He didn't think so, but he played along. 'I decline to answer that question on the grounds that it might incriminate me.'

'Come, come. No false modesty, please.' She lifted her head, listening to the music coming from the marquee, then shook her head. 'No, that's a waltz. Everyone can waltz. Can you foxtrot?'

'Hasn't that been banned?' he enquired.

'Too advanced for you, hmm? How about a tango, then?'

'Without treading on your toes? That I couldn't guarantee. But give me a rose to clutch beneath my teeth and I'm willing to give it a try.'

Her laugh was wholehearted and her mouth didn't disappoint. 'Well, that's certainly the best offer I've had for quite a while, but don't panic. Nothing is getting me out of this chair for the rest of the evening.'

He frowned. He'd escaped the marquee once he'd done his duty, fully intent on leaving, but what was *she* doing out here on her own?

'Is it such hard work being a best woman?' he asked.

'You wouldn't believe how tough. The hen party was an epic of organisation, and a bride doesn't get to look that perfect without someone to ensure she gets the attention she deserves on her big day.'

He followed her gaze to where the bride stood arm-in-arm at the entrance to the marquee with her groom, getting some air, chatting to friends. 'You did a great job. Guy's a lucky man,' he said.

'He deserves his luck. And Fran deserves him.'

That had been said with feeling, and he glanced back at her. 'You're close?'

'More like sisters than cousins,' she agreed. 'We're

both only children from the kind of dysfunctional families
that give marriage a bad name.'

'Believe me, if you had a family like mine you'd realise
that's not all bad news,' he assured her. Then, because he
didn't want to go there, he said, 'I'll go and fetch that
Scotch.'

Matty didn't take her eyes off Sebastian Wolseley as he
walked away from her. Tall, wide-shouldered, with beautifully cut dark hair that lifted in tiny ruffles in the light
breeze, he might have stepped from any woman's fantasy.
And his eyes changed from a dull slate to deep blue-green
when he smiled—like the sea when the sun shone.

He was a pleasure to look at, and she'd been watching
him ever since he'd slipped late into the reception. Seen
the warmth with which he'd been greeted by Guy. But,
although he was present in body, he'd clearly been somewhere else in spirit.

'Matty...' Toby, her cousin's three-year-old son,
pushed between her and the circular table, dragging at the
floor-length cloth and causing mayhem amongst the
glasses as he leaned against her knees, laying his head on
her lap. 'Hide me.'

'From what?'

'Connie. She says I have to go to bed.'

She rescued Sebastian's glass as it rolled towards the
edge of the table, spilling champagne in a wide semicircle
as it went. The stem was still warm from his hand...

'Have you had a good day?' she asked, setting it upright, giving her full attention to Toby.

He yawned. 'Mmm.'

He was already half asleep and she looked around, hoping to see Fran's housekeeper, Connie. He wouldn't have
given her the slip so easily before the arrival of his baby

sister, but he was no longer the dead centre of his small world. Maybe, overwhelmed by an occasion when his mother was the focus of attention, he needed a little one-to-one reassurance.

Ignoring the smears of chocolate decorating his cheek, she lifted him up onto her lap, nestling him against her shoulder.

'You know, you did a great job today, taking care of the rings. I was so proud of you.'

He snuggled closer. 'I didn't drop them, did I?'

'No.' She gave him a hug. 'You were a star.'

Sebastian walked up a shallow ramp into an inviting room softly lit by a single lamp. On the left was a drawing board, a computer workstation—a mini studio lit by a floor-to-ceiling window.

Matty Lang was an artist? He looked around, half expecting to see her work on the walls, but she favoured woven fabric hangings rather than conventional pictures. Or maybe that was her medium. There was nothing on the drawing board to give him a clue.

There was something about the set-up that didn't look quite right, but what with jet lag, an excess of family disapproval at the funeral and the realisation that while it was possible to dispense with the *'noblesse'*, the *'oblige'* was inescapable, his wits were not at their sharpest.

Whisky, on top of the single glass of champagne he'd drunk to toast the memory of George, was probably not his wisest move, but he wasn't driving and, since wisdom was not going to change anything, he might as well behave like a fool. It wouldn't be the first time.

On his right there was a large sofa, angled to look into the garden. It was flanked with end tables—one loaded

with books, the other with the remotes for a small television set and hi-fi unit.

It looked desperately inviting, and he would have given
a lot just to surrender to its comfort and stretch out for
five minutes, eyes closed. He resisted the temptation and
instead poured a small amount of Scotch into two glasses.
He walked into the kitchen, took mineral water from the
fridge and added a splash to both glasses before carrying
them back outside.

And immediately he saw what, if he hadn't been so
involved in his own problems, he should have noticed
from the beginning. What the ramp—instead of a step—
should have alerted him to.

Realised what had been missing from her workstation.
But then why would she need a conventional chair?
Because the reason Matty Lang wasn't dancing had noth-
ing to do with exhaustion from her best woman duties.

It was because she was in a lightweight, state-of-the art
wheelchair.

The tablecloth, which had hidden the wheels from the
casual observer, had been pulled askew, and for a moment
he hesitated, lost in a confusion of embarrassment, as he
remembered asking her if she tap-danced, and sheer admiration for her completely unfazed response.

He'd enjoyed her sense of humour, but now he could
appreciate it for what it truly was. Not just dry, but
wicked, as she'd teased him about his invitation to dance.
Precious little self-pity there.

She glanced up and caught him staring. Made a tiny
moue with her lips, acknowledging the truth.

'I'm not sure I should be giving you this,' he said,
handing her a glass. 'I wouldn't want you to get a ticket
for being drunk-in-charge. Especially since you've got a
passenger on board.'

She took a sip, rewarded him with a smile for not losing his head and bolting and, hampered by the child she was holding, gave him back the glass. 'Can you put that on the table for me?' Then, 'Have you met Toby?'

'No, I haven't had that pleasure…' He put down the glasses and folded himself up so that he was on the boy's level. 'Although I've heard all about you.' He offered his hand. 'I'm Sebastian. How d'you do?'

The child took his hand and shook it formally. 'I'm Toby Dymoke,' he said. 'Twice.'

'Twice?'

'It was my daddy's name, and it's my new daddy's name, too.'

'Well, that's handy. Not having to remember a new one.'

'They were brothers. I'm a brother, too. I've got a baby sister.'

'Really? Me too. At least, I've got three of them, although they're not babies any more. Great, isn't it?'

'Great,' Toby said, and with an expert wriggle slid down. 'I'm going to find her now.' And he ran off.

There was a momentary silence. Then Matty said, 'You have three sisters?'

'Three *older* sisters, actually. Bossy, Pushy and Lippy.'

'Not that great, then?'

'Hardly the hero-worshipping kind who trailed after me, the way they do in the storybooks,' he admitted.

'They gave you a hard time?'

'Gave? You should have been at George's funeral. Just because I'm his executor they blame me for the "entire tasteless performance". I'm quoting, you understand.'

'I understand.'

She had a way of not smiling, but making you feel as if she was. Inside.

'And for the fact that there was no dry sherry.'

She pulled her lips back in an attempt to stop herself from laughing out loud, then apologised. 'I'm sorry. It's not at all funny.'

'It should have been.' He thought, actually, that if she'd been there to share the joke it would have been bearable.

'What about your parents?' she asked, distracting him.

'What? Oh, my mother looked tragic and drank the champagne; my father harrumphed and said that it was a bit of a rum do.'

'And your sisters were a complete embarrassment?'

'Nothing new there.'

'While you, of course, were always the perfect brother. No frogspawn in their face cream, no spiders in their slippers, no itching powder in their beds.'

'Frogspawn in their face cream?'

'Forget I said that. That one is reserved for wicked stepmothers.'

'You did that to your stepmother?'

'Oh, I did all of them. But then I'm not nice.'

'That rather depends on what prompted it.'

'My father married her, poor woman. That was enough.' Then, when he didn't respond, 'I told you. I'm not nice.'

He shook his head and, taking his cue from her about being direct, unemotional, he said, 'It wasn't your character I was thinking about. It just occurred to me that if you managed to fish for frogspawn you can't always have been in a wheelchair.'

'You think a wheelchair would have stopped me? If I couldn't have managed it myself, I would have persuaded someone else to get it for me.'

'Fran?' he asked, glancing in the direction of the bride,

who smiled at him before leaning close to Guy to whisper something in his ear.

'I wouldn't have told her why I wanted it,' she assured him. 'She is much nicer than me. But it wasn't necessary. The wheelchair has only been part of my life since a combination of speed, black ice and an absence of due care and attention led to a close encounter with a brick wall.'

There was no self-pity in her words. It was a throwaway line with a matching smile—a practised defence against unwanted sympathy, he guessed—and she did it so well that he knew most people would grab at the opportunity to smile with her and move on.

Having seen what she could really do with a smile when she meant it, he wanted to know what had really happened—what she really felt.

'How long?' he asked.

'Three years.' And for a moment he glimpsed something the smile was supposed to hide. Not the three years that had passed, but the lifetime to come. Then, filling the silence while he thought about that, she said, 'Don't look so tragic. It could have been a lot worse.'

Forcing himself to match her matter-of-factness, he replied, 'Of course it could. You could be dead.' And then, remembering that momentary glimpse of something darker between the smiles, he wondered.

But Matty laughed, provoked out from behind the lurking shadows. 'Cheery soul, aren't you? Actually, I was being rather more down-to-earth about my condition.' Seeing his confusion, she grinned. 'It's an incomplete lower spine injury, which means I can at least use the bathroom just like anyone else.'

'Oh, well, I can see how that's a bonus. Although you'd have been in trouble if you'd been a man.'

She laughed out loud. 'I like you, big-shot banker. Most

of the people here would have taken to their heels by now.'

'Is that why you do it?'

'Do what?' she enquired innocently.

'Test people?'

'I only test the patronising ones who talk over my head. The ones who ask Fran if it's okay for me to have a drink—as if, because I can't stand up, I'm incapable of carrying on a normal conversation. The ones who speak to me as if I'm hard of hearing.'

He glanced around at the empty terrace and then back at her. 'You seem to have got it down to a fine art.'

'Lots of practice. But once we get this far I do like to get the bathroom thing out of the way, since sooner or later people start to worry about it. I find being open and direct makes for a more relaxing conversation.'

'Liar. You just want to make them squirm.'

'Are you squirming?'

'What do you think?' Then, 'How about sex?'

'Now?' she asked, as if he'd just propositioned her. 'I thought you were a man who liked to get to know a woman first.'

'I'm open to persuasion. So, is it a problem?'

'Nothing is a problem if you want it badly enough, Sebastian. For instance, I'm assured that, if I was prepared to strap myself into braces and put myself through several circles of hell, I could get up off my backside and stand on my own two feet. Even walk, after a fashion, although no one is promising it would be much fun, or even a remotely practical way to get about. Nothing as simple, or graceful, as my chair.' Again there was that wry little smile. 'And if you can't tango, what's the point?'

He didn't buy that, not for a minute, but she'd changed the subject and he didn't press it. Instead, picking up the lead she'd trailed to draw him away from the dark side of her life and back into the light, he asked, 'What would you have done if I'd been up for the foxtrot?'

'Oh, please! Most men's eyes glaze over at the first mention of a simple waltz.'

'You didn't give me a chance to glaze,' he objected.

'No, but then I was certain a man like you would know that you can smooch to a waltz. No one under sixty has the first idea how to foxtrot,' she went on, 'so I knew I was safe with that one.'

'So, we delay the dance until you've decided that I'm worth the effort. I'll just call a cab and we'll go somewhere quiet for dinner.'

Even as he took out his cellphone it occurred to him that he had no idea if she could manage a cab. Or whether any of the restaurants he knew were wheelchair accessible. And while he hesitated, confronted by a reality that was quite new to him, Guy came to his rescue.

'Matty, Fran wants you in the marquee. Apparently she's got some journalist slavering to look at that alphabet book you made for Toby.'

'She's what? It's her wedding reception, for heaven's sake!'

'Hey, don't blame me. I'm just the messenger. Since she's discovered how good she is at business I get the feeling that nothing is going to stop her from taking over the world.'

'I know,' she said, backing away from the table. 'To be honest I find it just a little bit scary.'

As Sebastian moved to accompany her, Guy, hand on his shoulder, detained him. 'Oh, no. My lovely wife has plans for you, too.' Then, as if suddenly aware that he'd interrupted something, 'You don't mind if I borrow him for a moment, do you, Matty?'

'You can keep him, darling. I've been neglecting my duties for long enough.' She extended her hand in a gesture that clearly said goodbye. 'Lovely to meet you, Sebastian.'

He held it rather than shook it. 'I thought we were going to have dinner?'

'Thanks, but it's been a long day. Next time you're in London, perhaps.' As if to emphasise her dismissal, she disentangled her fingers and, with a little wave, said, 'Try and be kinder to your sisters; I'm sure you needed bossing. And give my love to New York.'

She didn't wait for a response, but executed a neat ninety-degree turn and moved swiftly along the path. He watched her until she had been swallowed up in the crowd of people milling around the entrance, then he turned back to Guy.

'She's some woman.'

'Yes, she is. I'm sorry if I broke up something...'

'No. You heard her. We'll have dinner next time I'm in London.'

Guy grinned. 'She doesn't know you're staying?'

'I don't believe I mentioned it.'

Most people had deserted the gathering dusk of the garden for the flower-scented warmth of the marquee, and Matty paused for a moment in the entrance, assailed by a sudden ache in her throat as she watched couples wrapped in each other's arms swaying to the music.

She had so loved to dance. Loved the intimacy of being close to a man, her arms about his neck, while he whispered hot desire in her ear.

She shivered a little, looked back to where she'd been sitting. But as the crowd shifted she could see that the terrace was empty and, as she remembered the whispered exchange between Guy and Francesca, it took all her will-power to resist the feeling that Sebastian had sent out some kind of 'rescue me' signal.

She'd liked him. Wanted to believe he was better than that. And dinner, once, would have been special. But then he'd have gone away. And even if he hadn't—

'There you are,' Fran said, appearing at her side, saving her from her thoughts. 'Susie Palmer, the reporter who wrote that first piece about my business, wants to meet you—talk about Toby's alphabet book.'

'You gave her a copy?'

'Forgive me for being a smug mother, but I wanted her to know that you'd made the original for Toby.'

'If I was Toby's mother I'd be smug. Has Connie found him, by the way? He was running around in his pyjamas a little while ago.'

'Forget Toby for a moment. This woman has it in her power to give you the kind of publicity money can't buy.'

She wanted to tell Fran that she didn't want any kind of publicity. She wanted to say, *Don't do this to me. I'm not you...*

But her cousin was glowing with happiness, wanting so much to include her in her joy, so instead she smiled and said, 'Well, don't just stand there. Lead the way.'

CHAPTER TWO

'FOREST FAIRIES?'

Sebastian closed his eyes. Maybe this was all a bad dream, he thought. Maybe, if he concentrated very hard, he'd wake up in the pastel-free zone of his loft apartment...

Nothing doing.

When he opened them, the display of neon-bright, fairy-bedecked birthday cards was still there.

A week ago he'd been sitting in his Wall Street office, the fate of major corporations in his hands. All it had taken was one phone call to change his life from the American dream to a British farce. He just wished Matty Lang were here to see what the 'big-shot New York banker' had come to.

She, he was certain, would have enjoyed the joke. With her there he might have been able to see it for himself.

'They were our most profitable line...'

Blanche Appleby, Uncle George's secretary since time immemorial, hesitated, unsure exactly how to address Sebastian now that he was a head taller than her and, in his real life, the vice-president of an international bank.

He let the image of Matty's smile fade. 'It's still Sebastian, Blanche.'

She relaxed a little. 'It's been a good many years since I called you that.'

'I know, but you don't have to go all formal on me just because I've grown a few feet. I'm still going to need you to hold my hand on this one. I know nothing about the

26

greeting card business.' Knew nothing and cared less. But he was stuck with it.

'What about the staff?'

'I'll talk to them all later, when I have a better idea what's—'

'No. What do you want them to call you?'

He stifled a groan. Life was so much simpler in the US. There he was simply Sebastian Wolseley, a man defined by what he did and how well he did it rather than by the fact that one of his ancestors had been the mistress of Britain's merriest monarch.

As Viscount Grafton, his title was a courtesy one, one of his father's spares, passed on at birth to keep him going until he inherited the big one. He'd made damn sure that no one in New York knew about it. And perhaps that was a small upside.

Baiting minor aristocracy was a blood sport in the British media; any coverage of his involvement in Coronet Cards was likely to be of the mocking variety. Since it would be the Viscount they were mocking, he might just get away with it.

It would be worth any amount of mockery if it meant no one in New York discovered that he'd put his career at the bank temporarily on hold to rescue *Forest Fairies* from fiscal disaster.

'What did the staff call George?' he asked.

'Everyone but the senior staff just called him Mr George.'

Paternal respect for the Honourable George, what else?

'Maybe in another twenty years,' he said. 'For now I'd prefer it if everyone just called me Sebastian.'

'Everyone?' She sounded slightly shocked.

'If you'd pass that on.'

'Well, if that's what you want.'

'I do.' Then, since there was no point in putting off the

inevitable, he indicated the display of birthday cards, paper plates, napkins and balloons strewn across the conference table that took up one end of the office. 'You say these were Coronet's bestselling lines?'

Maybe he should have made more effort to hide his disbelief.

'You've never seen the television programme?' she asked, surprised.

'I don't believe so.'

'No, well, I don't suppose they're on American television.' Her tone suggested that their transatlantic cousins didn't know what they were missing. 'They were very popular here, which is why George bought a twenty-five-year licence to use the characters on a range of cards and party products.'

That got his attention. 'Did you say twenty-five?'

'*Forest Fairies* parties have been very popular with three- to six-year-old girls.'

'George bought the rights to produce this stuff for twenty-five years?' he persisted. 'How much did it cost the company?'

'It was a very good deal,' she said, instantly protective. 'The line was the mainstay of the business for several years.'

The fact that she appeared to be referring to all this success in the past tense finally got through. 'Was?'

'Sales have declined somewhat since the TV programme was dropped from the schedules,' she admitted.

Sebastian was torn between relief that there would be fewer *Forest Fairies* in the world and despair that the one item keeping the company afloat was in decline.

It was a close call.

Distracted by a howl of frustration, Matty gave up any pretence of working. All morning she'd been stopping her mind from wandering off to think about Sebastian Wolseley. The sexy way his eyes had creased as his face had relaxed into a smile. The way his eyes changed colour.

Back in New York, he'd still be asleep, and that was a tantalising thought, too. It was so easy to imagine him lying with his face in a pillow, his long limbs spread-eagled across a wide bed.

She saw him in one of those vast loft apartments, with light flooding in from floor-to-ceiling windows across acres of floor space, 'An Englishman in New York' playing on an expensive stereo.

And she smiled. So few people were able to handle the wheelchair without embarrassment, but he'd passed every test with flying colours.

The journalist who'd been so anxious to interview her about her work hadn't been able to get away fast enough. Promising to phone. And maybe she would. 'Plucky wheelchair-bound woman illustrates cute book...' had to be a bigger story than one about just any ordinary, able-bodied woman illustrating a cute book.

Or maybe it had been her fault. Maybe the woman's carefully phrased questions had been in such sharp contrast to Sebastian's matter-of-fact attitude that she'd been unusually difficult. Prickly, even.

But for a few minutes he'd talked to her as if she was whole. Saying things that no one else would have dreamed of saying. Asking her if she tap-danced...

And even when he'd realised that tap-dancing was not, never would be, part of her repertoire he hadn't changed—hadn't started talking to her as if she was witless. Dinner with him would have been a rare pleasure. Sitting at a candlelit table, she could have pretended for a few dizzy hours that on the outside she was like any other woman. The way she was deep inside. With the same longings. The same desire to be loved, to have a man hold her, make love to her.

She closed her eyes for a moment, shutting out the reminders that she was not, would never be, like other women. How dared he joke with her, talk as if she could get up and dance as soon as she made the effort?

Then, with a deep breath, she opened them again. It was unfair to blame him. She'd seen him staring into his glass as if into an abyss and just hadn't been able to keep her mouth shut. She'd only got herself to blame for her disturbed nights.

Because it wasn't just this morning that she'd been thinking about him. He'd been there, in her head, since the moment he'd taken her hand, held it a touch too long. Been there the minute she'd stopped concentrating on something else.

But Monday was a working day. She couldn't afford to allow her mind to wander when she had a tight deadline, and she picked out a fresh pastel and concentrated on the illustration in front of her.

'Go on, Toby, you can do it!'

She looked up again just in time to catch Toby's attempt at scaling the brightly coloured climbing frame set up in the garden. It was a bit of a stretch, and he was finding it frustratingly hard to reach the top. She leaned forward in her chair, physically encouraging him with her body, yearning to be out there, giving him the boost he needed. Her frustration, unable to find any other outlet, vented itself on the paper in front of her, and with a few swift strokes of the colour in her hand Hattie Hot Wheels, her cartoon alter ego, was lunging from her wheelchair, arms outstretched, as she flew to Toby's side, scooping him up and lifting him up.

Another triumph for her superheroine, whose special

powers allowed her to convert frustrated helplessness into action…

Then Fran placed a steadying hand at Toby's back, in case he should falter, smiling encouragement, and, putting in a big effort, he finally made it. Of course he did. Why would Toby need a fantasy superheroine when he had a mother with two good arms and legs?

'Matty!' Toby, spotting her from his vantage point, wobbled as he gave her an ecstatic two-armed wave from the top, and her heart rose to her throat. 'Look at me!'

'Oh, bravo, Toby!' she called, waving back. 'How did you get all the way up there?'

'I climbed. All by myself.'

'No!' she said, doing the whole amazed thing. 'But it's so high! How did you do it?'

'Do you want to see?' he asked.

'You betcha I want to see.'

And by the time he'd done it for a third time, just to prove to his apparently sceptical godmother that it wasn't just a fluke, he could indeed manage it 'all by himself'.

Her smile faded as she saw the half-finished picture she'd just ruined with her cartoon. Deliberate vandalism? Or was that just a load of psychological mumbo-jumbo?

She'd illustrated dozens of romantic stories for women's magazines, and while she'd known from the beginning that this one—a wide, deserted beach with the distant lovers silhouetted against the setting sun—was going to be tough, she was a professional. This was her living, and she couldn't afford to turn down commissions just because they tugged at painful memories.

'Come and join us, Matty,' Fran called, encouraging her to play truant. 'It's going to rain tomorrow.'

It was hard to resist such siren calls, but every minute spent with Toby was a wrenching reminder of how much she'd lost in the split-second lapse that had robbed her of that future. And Fran's new baby, joy that she was, just made things worse.

Matty was beginning to feel as if she was trapped on the wrong side of the glass, a spectator to a life she was denied. If only she could afford to move away, get out of London and make a new kind of life. One that wasn't just a fantasy.

When the phone began to ring, it was almost a relief to call back, 'Maybe later,' before turning to pick up the receiver.

'Matty Lang.'

'Hello, Matty Lang.'

For a moment her heart seemed to stop beating. It was as if her mind, conjuring up the image of the sleeping man, had somehow woken him.

When it started again, very slowly, she said, 'Hello, Sebastian Wolseley.' Then, 'You're an early riser. Isn't it some unearthly hour of the morning in New York?'

'That is true. But here in London it's just coming up to eleven o'clock.'

No, well, she hadn't really thought he was calling from the other side of the Atlantic just to say hello. That would have been totally ridiculous.

'You said you'd have dinner with me when I came back, but I wondered if you might be able to make lunch? I've booked a table at Giovanni's.'

Giovanni's? A restaurant so famous that it didn't have to bother with anything as functional as an address. The kind of restaurant where the rich and famous went to be seen. And it was nearly eleven now.

She had two hours to shower, change, find a parking space. Her hair! She…

She was living in cloud-cuckoo land. Getting carried away.

She never went anywhere without checking it out first.

Calling the restaurant to make sure it was wheelchair accessible. That the cloakroom wasn't upstairs. That, even if it was on the ground floor, she wouldn't get stuck in the loo door.

Okay, she could still do that.

But she wouldn't.

'I said perhaps,' she reminded him. 'When you came back. You haven't been anywhere.'

'On the contrary, I went to Sussex yesterday,' he said, and she could see the teasing spark that would be lighting his eyes, the tiny lift at the corner of his mouth that presaged a smile. 'Command invitation to lunch with the family.'

'Why is it that I find it hard to believe that you'd respond to anyone's command?'

'Well, I did want to borrow a car.'

'Your family has spare cars lying around?'

'It's old. Just taking up space in the garage. I wish I'd taken you with me.'

'I'm jolly glad you didn't.'

'You're right. Dead boring. Utterly selfish to even consider it. So, anyway, I've been somewhere, and now I'm back.'

'You know I didn't mean that.'

'I don't recall you stipulating a destination. Doesn't Sussex count?'

It counted. That was the problem. She wanted to have lunch with him.

It would be so easy, sitting opposite him, surrounded by luxury, pretending that they were just two people having lunch together. But then he'd get up and walk away.

She'd already had that dream, but then she'd woken up.

'I'm really sorry, Sebastian, but I've got a deadline that's getting tighter by the minute. I'm afraid lunch today will have to be a sandwich. But thank you for asking.'

And then, before he could say anything else, she gently replaced the receiver on the cradle.

Sebastian sat back and acknowledged that he could have handled that better.

Giovanni's, it occurred to him, had been his first mistake.

He'd really wanted to see her, talk to her, but instead of saying so he'd thrown out an invitation to lunch with him at a moment's notice at the fanciest restaurant he could think of. Few women of his acquaintance could have resisted.

But she wasn't like other women, and he hadn't given a single thought as to what she might prefer. Or even that she might have a full and busy life without a moment to spare for him.

Nothing new there. He'd been treating women in that casual, take it or leave it manner for years.

The decent women had left it, the minute they realised he wasn't offering more. Only the users had hung around: the ones who'd wanted to be seen in smart restaurants, mixing with high-stake players. And that had been just fine. Everyone had got what they wanted without the bother of pretending that they were engaging in anything but the most superficial of relationships.

Nothing messy to interfere with the only thing that really mattered to him. His career.

'Sebastian, is your phone off the hook?' Blanche asked, then, seeing him sitting with the receiver in his hand, 'Oh, you're making a call.'

He looked up. 'It's finished,' he said, replacing the receiver. 'What can I do for you?'

'Our biggest buyer wants to set up a meeting with you. George always used to take him out to lunch, make a fuss of him.'

'That sounds like fun. What do we talk about?'

'Next year's range.'

'Have we got one? Why haven't I seen it?'

The way she lifted her shoulders spoke volumes.
'George let things go a bit towards the end.' She sat down
rather suddenly in the chair facing his desk. 'I still can't
get used to not seeing him…' She waved in his direction
as she groped for a handkerchief in her pocket.

'I'm sorry, Blanche, you worked for George for a long
time. This must be hard for you.'

'I was very fond of him. He was a gentleman.'

He wondered if she'd be quite so warm towards him if
she knew about the gaping hole in the pension fund. He
fervently hoped she'd never have to find out.

'You can't know how grateful we all are that the family
has decided to keep the company going. They were never
actually enthusiastic about it—the company—were they?'

'Not exactly,' he agreed. 'But then they were never
exactly enthusiastic about George, either.'

George hadn't had to work, but he'd never been content
to play the role he'd been born to. Had had no taste for
hunting, shooting or fishing.

They'd had that—along with so much else—in common.

'We all thought the company would be wound up,' she
went on, 'and obviously we'd have understood. Business
hasn't exactly been booming in the last couple of years.
But it would have meant early retirement for most of us.
I know some people can't wait, but not me. What on earth
would I do with myself?'

There were worse things than early retirement,
Sebastian thought. But if he could get the business back
to the point where he could find a buyer and use to the
money to fund annuities for the staff, she and the rest
of George's loyal staff would never have to face that
prospect.

'You can imagine how pleased we all were when we heard you were going to step into the breach, so to speak.'

'Yes, well, there won't be any business unless we do something about next year's range. Where do we start?'

'It's a bit late. The lead time for orders—'

'Blanche, if I'm going to buy this man an expensive lunch, I'd like to have something to sell him while he's feeling replete and satisfied.' She didn't exactly leap in with suggestions. 'Where do new designs come from?' he asked. 'Did George ever commission an artist to come up with a high-concept design that could be developed into a range of products? Or did he rely on them to come to him?'

'He hasn't commissioned anything in a while, but George had a lot of contacts. He always managed to come up with something.'

'That isn't a lot of help to me.'

'No. I'm sorry.' She gave herself a little shake. 'You could look in George's ideas cabinet.' She gestured in the direction of a plan chest, tucked away in the corner of the office. 'He sometimes bought things he thought would be useful and tucked them away. For a rainy day, he used to say. I guess it's here.' And this time her tears overflowed.

'Why don't you go and have a cup of tea, or something, while I check it out?' he suggested, helping her to her feet and moving her towards the door, utterly helpless in the face of her grief.

'I'm so sorry…'

'It's okay. I understand. Really.' Unfortunately he understood only too well. 'Why don't you take an early lunch?'

He leaned back against the door for a moment. He hadn't realised until now that Blanche had been in love with George, too. But he'd bet any amount of money that the old rogue had been well aware of her feelings and had taken full advantage of them. Yet more pressure to come up with the goods.

He turned to the plan chest—not that he had any desire to examine its contents. He didn't even want to be in this country, but there was no point in putting off the inevitable.

The first drawer contained some old botanical drawings. Foxed, and a bit tattered at the edges, the only thing in their favour, as far as he could see, was that they were out of copyright by a century or two.

But what did he know?

The second drawer offered a series of brightly coloured nursery rhyme characters.

As he continued through the drawers he realised that he was doing no more than going through the motions.

He could look at a set of books and have a pretty fair idea of whether they belonged to a company on the way up or on the way out. Coronet Cards had been doing little more than ticking over for the last three years. If he'd been asked for an unbiased opinion, he'd have suggested either finding a buyer—a company who might be prepared to take over the company in order to add the Coronet trademark to their list—or winding it up before it began to make serious losses.

Since, for the moment, neither of those options was open to him, he had no choice but to try and turn it around. But it hadn't taken more than one morning in the office to realise that he needed help.

And, once again, it was Matty Lang's face that swam into view.

'Are you okay?'

Matty looked up from her second attempt at the beach scene. Fran was standing in the open doorway, her baby on her shoulder, her forehead wrinkled in a look of concern.

'I'm fine,' she lied. 'Or I would be if I could remember what a beach looked like.'

'We could open up the sandbox,' she offered. 'I'm sure Toby would be more than willing to refresh your memory.'

'Thanks, but I think I'll pass on that one. Where is he?'

'Baking with Connie. Brownies, I think.'

'Thanks for the warning.'

'Her cooking has improved a lot,' Fran chided, but with a grin.

'So why are you hiding out down here, interrupting me?'

The grin widened into laughter. 'Okay, I can take a hint. But don't work too hard.'

'Work?' With a broad gesture, Matty took in her drawing board and computer bench. 'You call this work? I sit here in the warm and dry, turning out pretty pictures for a living. What's so hard about that?'

'Even doing the things we love can get hard if we don't have a break, Matty.' Then, 'Why don't we all go down to the coast tomorrow so that you can refresh your memory?'

No…

'I thought you said it was going to rain tomorrow.'

'That was when I was trying to get you outside today. You look a bit pale. You did so much to make the blessing special for us. I can't help feeling that you overdid it.'

'What tosh. You should be away somewhere on a honeymoon, Mrs Dymoke, indulging in love's young dream with the gorgeous Guy instead of worrying about me.'

'Oh, please. We'd been married nearly a year before we managed the blessing and reception. At this rate we'll be love's pensioners before we get around to a honeymoon.'

'You should make some time for yourselves, Fran.'

'Just kidding. But it's a bad time to go away. Besides, why waste this lovely weather when we have the perfect excuse to escape to the sun in January?' She dropped a kiss on her sleeping babe's brow. 'And this little one will be more manageable by then, too.'

'It's going to be a family honeymoon?'

'Absolutely. But we're staying in a house belonging to someone Guy knows. It has a full complement of staff, apparently, and I've been assured that I shall not be called upon to change as much as a single nappy.'

'The best of all possible worlds, then. It sounds bliss.'

'It will be, but I wish—'

'You've got everything you could ever wish for, Fran,' Matty intervened, before her cousin could voice her guilt at leaving her behind. 'And for once I'll be able to get on with some work without having to put up with a constant stream of interruptions.' As if to mock her, her doorbell rang. 'Now what?'

She lifted the entryphone. 'Yes?'

'Meals on Wheels, ma'am. Since you wouldn't come to lunch with me, I've brought lunch to you.'

Fran's eyes widened. 'Is that Sebastian Wolseley?' she whispered.

'It must be,' Matty replied, with remarkable composure considering her insides had clenched into a nervous fist at the sound of his voice. 'He's the only man I've turned down lunch with today.'

'You did *what*?'

'Treat them mean, keep them keen,' she said, with a fair attempt at a laugh. Not that she imagined Fran was fooled for a minute by her apparent carelessness.

She shouldn't care, but it was a long time since she'd thought about a man—thought about a man in connection with herself, that was—for more than five minutes. She'd wasted a lot more than five minutes on Sebastian Wolseley, which suggested that she did. Care.

'It seems to be working,' her cousin replied, apparently amused. 'Is leaving him standing on the doorstep part of the plan?'

She was tempted. She'd said she was busy and he'd taken no notice. That was bad, wasn't it? He hadn't listened to what she was saying and that showed a lack of respect...or something.

The warmth spreading upwards towards her cheeks suggested that respect was the last thing she wanted from him.

That his unwillingness to take no for an answer was much more appealing.

Dangerous, but appealing, and she buzzed him in. Then, as Fran headed for the French windows, Matty said, 'Excuse me, just where do you think you're going?'

'You think I'm going to hang around and play gooseberry?' Fran asked, as Sebastian appeared from the hall and joined them. Then she gracefully extended a hand, accepting a kiss on her cheek, and said, 'Hello, Sebastian. How're you settling into the flat? Is there anything you need?'

'Everything's fine, thank you, Francesca. I'm very grateful to you. Even the most comfortable hotel loses its charm after a week.' He looked at the baby in her arms. 'This is Toby's sister, I take it?' He held out a finger for the baby to clutch.

Matty watched as Fran said, 'Say hello, Stephanie.' The baby blew a bubble and earned herself a full-throttle smile. 'Say goodbye, Stephanie.' Then, 'Guy will give you call later in the week to organise supper one evening soon.'

'I look forward to it.'

'And if you change your mind about tomorrow, Matty,

give me a call,' she said, before stepping out in the garden, leaving her alone with Sebastian.

'Tomorrow?' he asked, finally dragging his gaze from the lovely Madonna-like image of mother and child and turning to look directly at Matty.

She shrugged, reminding herself that it wasn't at all attractive to begrudge a baby one of his smiles. 'Fran suggested a day at the coast. I told her I was too busy. *She* listened.'

'I listened. You said you were planning a sandwich.' He offered her the kind of brown recycled paper carrier bag used by expensive organic bakers. 'I thought I'd save you the trouble of making it.'

She had two alternatives: keep looking at him, or take the carrier and look inside that. She took the carrier. And kept on looking at him.

'Is it my imagination,' she asked, after a silence that stretched seconds too long, 'or are sandwiches heavier than they used to be?'

'Not noticeably. But since I had no idea what you'd prefer—you might, for instance, be a vegetarian, or allergic to shellfish, or hate cheese—I thought I'd better bring a selection.'

'That was thoughtful.'

'I'm a thoughtful man. Ask anyone.'

She peeked into the carrier, because continuing to stare at him was not smart. It would give him the wrong idea—or possibly the right one; whichever it was, it wouldn't be good. Besides, looking at him was making her feel dizzy…

'I seem to be spoilt for choice,' she said, taking her time over her selection. Gathering her composure, the strength to dismiss him. The feelings he provoked in her pathetic body were too powerful to be ignored, laughed away. She had to protect herself. Send him away. Now.

She stared in the bag. There were more sandwiches than one person could eat in a week—even supposing that person ever wanted to eat again—but for some reason she couldn't read the labels clearly, so she picked out the first one that came to hand. She blinked and saw that it was smoked salmon with cream cheese on dark rye bread. The man had taste; she'd give him that.

'For future reference, Sebastian,' she said, as she placed it on the workbench beside her. 'In the unlikely event that you should ever be tempted to do this again. I'm not a vegetarian, I love shellfish, and I believe cheese to be the food of the gods.' Then, handing the carrier back to him, she dug deep for a smile and said, 'Thank you. Thoughtful indeed. I shall enjoy it later. When I've finished work.'

Then she quickly turned back to her drawing board in what she hoped he would understand was a gesture of dismissal. Brushed away a spot of something wet that landed on her drawing board. Waited for him to walk out of her life.

When he didn't take the hint—she hadn't really expected him to; if she were honest hadn't really wanted him to—she tried just a bit harder with, 'Can you find your own way out?'

CHAPTER THREE

SEBASTIAN shook his head. Not because finding his way out of her apartment was beyond him, but in total admiration of her insouciance.

Having been turned down for lunch, he'd gone out on a limb in his attempt to charm her but she still wasn't having any of it.

'You are a class act, Matty Lang.'

She had the grace to smile. 'Thank you.'

'Don't thank me. It wasn't a compliment.'

Except, of course, it was and they both knew it. He admired that kind of cool. Her ability to remain completely unimpressed by humility from a man not given to such gestures. Or maybe she recognised the truth: that he wasn't used to taking no for an answer.

'You won't object if I call a cab before you kick me out?' he asked, raising the stakes a little as he took out his cellphone.

'You came by cab?'

'No. Why? Do you have something against them?'

She pulled her lips tight against her teeth, as if trying very hard not to smile, trying very hard not change her mind and ask him to stay.

'Not at all,' she replied, once she had the smile under control. 'I just wondered why you didn't use your car. When you'd gone through such agony to acquire it. Of course you'd have got a parking ticket, but even so...'

'Actually, I walked...' Damn! No...

'Good for you. Why don't you just walk back?'

The smile, he could see, was making a bid for freedom. She'd enjoyed his discomfort. Would probably split her sides if he made an absolute idiot of himself trying to avoid touchy words like 'walk' as if they were landmines. Well, two could play at that game...

'I'd probably faint from lack of nourishment. But don't worry, I'll stand out in the street if you'd prefer.'

'After you've gone to such trouble to provide me with lunch?'

An errant dimple appeared just above the right-hand corner of her mouth.

'Would I be that unkind?' she asked.

'Apparently,' he said. 'If you were in the least bit grateful you'd have invited me to join you.'

She laid a hand against her heart and said, 'Oh, I'm so sorry. Did you want to stay?'

'Witch,' he said, quite unable to stop himself from laughing. But then, that was why he was here. Because even when he'd been at a truly low point she'd made him smile.

'That's better.'

'You prefer insults to charm?'

'Of course. Charm is so...easy. Insults, on the other hand, have an astringent, refreshing quality. So much more honest. Sit down; make your call.'

Better, he thought, making himself at home on her sofa, scrolling through the numbers stored in his phone as if looking for a cab company, but taking his time about it.

'So, is that the secret?' he asked, as if more absorbed in the phone than in her answer. 'I have to call you names if I want to spend a little time with you?'

'You get to make one phone call,' she told him. 'Conversation is not included.'

Matty wasn't fooled for a minute. Sebastian Wolseley

wasn't calling a cab, he was just going through the motions, spinning out the time, hoping she'd relent and ask him to stay.

Why?

What did he want from her?

Lunch, the sandwiches... He wouldn't be pushing it so hard unless he wanted something.

'I asked you to have dinner with me on Saturday,' he went on, as if he hadn't heard, 'and you dismissed me in favour of chatting up a journalist.'

He pressed the call button, waited. Disconnected.

'Engaged,' he said in response to her unspoken question. Then, looking up suddenly and catching her staring at him, 'I invite you for lunch at the most romantic restaurant in town and you say you're too busy. And you're not even going to invite me to stay and share your very brief lunch break, despite the fact that I provided the sandwiches.'

'You said it,' she replied. 'I'm a witch. For my next trick, if you're not out of here in thirty seconds, I turn you into a frog.'

'Are you sure about that?' He had the feeling she wasn't fooled by his phone act, so this time he hit dial before he lifted the phone to his ear. This time it really was engaged... 'Wouldn't you have to kiss me to reverse the spell?'

Matty wished that didn't sound so appealing. She was already finding it hard enough to stop herself from staring at his mouth. And now he'd put the idea into her head...

'Oh, for heaven's sake,' she said, abruptly changing the subject, desperate to drive the image from her mind. 'You can stop pretending to call a cab.'

'Pretending?' he exclaimed, all shock, horror. She was not impressed.

'Pretending. Since I've had nothing but interruptions all morning you might as well stay and eat one of those sandwiches. Then, when you've told me what you want, I'm kicking you out whether you have transport or not.'

'What makes you think I want anything but your company?'

'I can read minds, remember? I'll fetch some plates. Would you like something to drink?' she asked, manoeuvring her chair from behind the drawing board and heading for the kitchen.

'Actually, you'll find a bottle of perfectly chilled Sancerre on the kitchen table.'

'Sancerre?' She turned and gave him a stern look that suggested he was a piece of work.

He smiled back, acknowledging the fact, and said, 'I'd offer to come and open it, but I'm far too comfortable.'

Oh, that was good. She had to bite her lip to stop herself from grinning. 'You had no intention of leaving, did you?'

'No, but then we both know that you weren't really going to kick me out.'

'My mistake was in ever letting you in.'

'Once you answered the doorbell you had no choice.' Perhaps realising that being smug wasn't in his best interests, he quickly added, 'You could never bring yourself to be that rude.'

'I could,' she assured him, 'but I wouldn't have been. I can do an excellent impression of Fran's Greek live-in cook/housekeeper/nanny when I don't want to be disturbed.' And he surely disturbed her. 'All mangled English and incomprehension. It works a treat on unwanted callers.'

She found the corkscrew, opened the bottle and, grabbing a couple of plates, rejoined her uninvited guest.

'You'll find glasses in the sideboard,' she said. 'If it's

not too much trouble.' Then, as he unfolded himself from the sofa and opened the cupboard, 'What flat?'

'Flat?' he asked, setting out the glasses and taking the wine from her.

'Fran asked you if you'd settled into the flat.'

'Oh, right. Guy offered me the use of his old place until I find something permanent.'

'His old place?' Guy didn't have an 'old place'. 'Are you by any chance referring to his former home in a luxurious riverside penthouse?'

'Does he have two?'

She shook her head. 'I thought he was letting it on a short-term lease to some big corporation.'

'He was. It's between tenants at the moment. That's what he dragged me away for on Saturday. To give me the key.'

'Oh.' She mentally apologised for even thinking that he might have sent out a 'rescue me' signal to Guy. Then, 'You really are *good* friends, aren't you?' She fetched the sandwich she'd chosen and rolled her chair up to the table as he helped himself to one from the carrier.

'That's what I said.'

'Can you open that drawer and get out a couple of knives?' she asked. He passed one to her. 'Thank you. And some napkins.' Then, 'You *said* you were going back to New York.'

'I'm quite certain that I didn't. I'm not going anywhere until I've sorted out the mess George bequeathed me.'

'And is that going to take a week, two weeks…?' She stopped, afraid of showing that she gave a damn—terribly afraid that she did—and concentrated on opening the package containing her sandwich with fingers that were quite suddenly all thumbs.

'I'm not sure how long it's going to take,' he said,

following her example but with considerably more success. 'I've got six months' compassionate leave from the bank. If it takes longer I guess I'll be looking for another job.'

She finally gave up on the sandwich and looked at him. 'Six months? Good grief, it must be some mess.'

He took her sandwich from her, opened it and passed it back. 'It's one of the reasons I turned up on your doorstep uninvited. I was hoping for some advice.'

'Advice?'

Well, for heaven's sake, Matty Lang, you knew he wanted something other than a little light conversation over lunch. But disappointment settled, leaden, in the pit of her stomach.

'What kind of advice?' she asked, then bit into the sandwich. It tasted of nothing.

Sebastian poured out two glasses of wine. At least Matty hadn't dismissed the notion of helping him as a concept. And she hadn't queried the other reasons, which was perhaps just as well, since he wasn't too sure about them himself.

'Guy told me that you're an illustrator,' he said. 'I wondered if you know anything about the greetings card business.'

Her forehead creased in a bemused frown. 'Greetings cards?'

'Happy Birthday, Happy Mother's Day, Happy Anything-you-care-to-name Day.'

'That was your cousin's business?'

'George founded Coronet Cards when he was at art school, producing small quantities of *avant-garde* cards using his own and his friends' work—more to help them out than anything.'

She pushed aside her disappointment. 'Coronet? I know

them. Aren't some of their early cards collectors' items now?'

'I believe so. What a pity he didn't get his fellow students to sign contracts so that we could reissue them.' He shrugged. 'He was never that great a businessman. Maybe he should have stuck to painting.'

'Was he any good?'

He smiled. 'No.'

'Oh. And now Coronet is in trouble?'

'It's more complicated than that. George got into a bit of a muddle with the finances in the last few years.'

'So you've put your career on hold for six months to rescue it?' She propped her elbows on the table and her chin on her knuckles. 'You'll forgive me if I suggest that sounds like serious overkill.'

'You think so?'

'Of the sledgehammer to crack a walnut variety.' Perhaps deciding that she had overstepped an invisible line, she sat back, broke a piece off her sandwich, but didn't eat it.

'Go on,' he said.

She lifted her shoulders slightly, as if embarrassed by what she was about to say. 'Coronet has class, but it isn't exactly a major player in the greetings card industry. Hardly the kind of company to merit six months of a Wall Street banker's time.'

His only response was to take a bite out of his beef and horseradish sandwich.

'If it's that much of a mess,' she went on, presumably encouraged by his silence, 'surely it would have been wiser to leave a competent accountant to wind it up?' She lifted a pair of expressive brows, inviting him to contradict her. When he didn't, she said, 'Obviously not. So what am I missing?'

'Nothing.' He shrugged. 'You're right, of course, but unfortunately winding up the company is not an option. When I said that George got into a bit of a muddle, I might have been understating the problem.'

'I'm sorry. I didn't mean to pry,' she said, hands spread as if to ward off any suggestion that she was in the slightest bit interested. 'It's absolutely none of my business.'

'I'm asking for advice, help, and you have every right to know what you're getting into.' He hadn't intended to tell her any of this, but he needed someone he could talk to. An ally. Every instinct assured him that Matty was that person. 'The truth is, Matty, that there's a great big hole in the company finances where the pension fund should be.'

'Oh.' Then, 'Should you be telling me that?'

'No. Should it leak out the papers will have a field-day at my family's expense, the company will go into receivership and a lot of very good people who worked for George for years will face a bleak retirement. The last of those things concerns me most.'

'I see what you meant when you said he was "bad".'

'I was referring to his numerous wives and even more numerous lovers.'

'An expensive habit.'

'Even so, he would never have stolen from people who worked for him. I'm afraid it was his last wife who did the damage. An agency nurse who took care of him after he'd had a heart bypass. Florence Nightingale incarnate until he'd placed a ring on her finger. The yawning gap in the pension fund and her departure appear to have occurred at about the same time. But I can't prove anything, and even if I could the money would probably never be recovered—at least not in time to do any good. There's nothing to be gained from pursuing her, only scandal, and I don't want George remembered as a sad old fool.'

'No, of course you don't.' Her hand came to rest momentarily on his. Then, whisking it away to curl her fingers through her hair, leaving it standing up in a lopsided crest, she said, 'But won't that kind of money take years to replace?'

'My aim is to get the company back on track. I plan to junk the dead wood, bring in some great new designs, then sell out to one of the big companies and use the proceeds to fund redundancies and an early retirement package for the older staff.'

'''*With a single bound he was free…*''' She stopped toying with the sandwich, having apparently lost interest in lunch. 'I'm afraid that if you asked me out to lunch in the hopes that I could rustle up a few brilliant designs over coffee you're going to be disappointed.'

Now he'd really offended her. Sticking to business wasn't going to work either, it seemed. Maybe he should just go for the truth.

'It wasn't, Matty. It isn't. The truth is, it's not just advice I wanted. I've spent a somewhat surreal morning discussing the future of *Forest Fairies* and I wanted to tell you about it. I knew you'd see the funny side of it.' He looked directly at her. 'I hoped maybe you could help me to see it, too.'

'Oh?' Still not impressed. 'So why didn't you just say so?'

'I don't usually have to give a reason when I invite a woman out to lunch,' he admitted, risking a smile. 'I've never had to work this hard for a date before.'

'No,' she said, somewhat wryly, 'I'm sure you haven't.' She changed the subject. '*Forest Fairies*? Aren't they the ones on television? Dressed in the kind of inappropriate day-glo colours that would stand out a mile and guarantee any genuine fairy a front-page spread in a supermarket tabloid? Right under the story about aliens landing in Hyde Park.'

He laughed. 'You see? I knew you could do it.'

Her own face softened. 'You should laugh more often, Sebastian. It's good for the soul.'

'I'll remind you of that,' he said, 'the next time I ask you out.'

For a moment they just looked at one another, and smiling was the last but one thing on his mind. Just in front of talking business.

Right up there at the front of the queue was a sharp desire to reach out and lay his hand against the downy softness of her cheek, feel her lean into his palm. Just that.

The feeling left him floundering, vulnerable, and just a little helpless. He usually dated women with long shiny hair, soft curves and high, high heels. Women who, temporarily, looked good on his arm and, when he replaced them without a backward glance, usefully added to his reputation for ruthlessness.

He suspected Matty knew that.

Suspected that she thought him shallower than a puddle. Was certain that she wouldn't waste a moment fulfilling his fantasies. Knew that he would be wise to keep his hands—and his thoughts—to himself. He didn't want rejecting him to become a habit for her.

Much more sensible to stick to business.

'Let's stick to the fairies,' she said, breaking eye contact. And apparently reading his mind again. 'What's your problem with them?'

'George paid a fortune for a twenty-five-year licence to turn them into birthday cards, gift wrap, party goods and anything else he could think of, in the blissful assumption that they'd go on for ever. Unfortunately television is a here-today-and-gone-tomorrow medium, and the fairies have been dumped in favour of a whole new set of creatures.'

'And you need something exciting to take their place?'

'Before next week.'

'Next week! You're kidding.' He didn't move a muscle. 'You're not kidding. So what's happening next week?'

'I have to take our biggest buyer out to lunch and show him the new season's offerings. He'll probably reorder the standards—the ''aunty'' cards—because one bunch of pansies or daisies looks very much like another. But I have to have something new for the kindergarten market.'

'Surely there's someone in the company who sources material for you?'

'There was. We buried him on Saturday.'

'Boy, you are in trouble,' she said, reaching for the bottle and topping up his glass. 'Have another of these excellent sandwiches.' Then, 'You've really got nothing?'

'Some old-fashioned nursery rhyme designs that wouldn't impress a two-year-old.'

'So how did you think I could help?'

'I don't know. I just needed to talk to someone who isn't involved. The Coronet staff are all on edge, afraid they're going to lose their jobs, the family are terrified of a scandal—'

'And they're all expecting you to save them?'

'Oh, please. Don't make me out to be some kind of hero, racing to the rescue. I have a reputation to think of.'

'Not to mention the family name,' she said, but with just enough of a hint of irony to take the sting out of the words. 'That's a lot of pressure.'

'Pressure I can handle. But this needs something else.

Something I haven't got.' Then, 'Don't you do children's illustrations?'

'Not the kind of high-concept stuff you're talking about. If the television people have moved on, can't you licence the latest fad?'

'They've already been snapped up by the big companies with even bigger wallets. No, I've got to start my own must-have fad.'

'In a week?'

'I know. It's ridiculous. But I have to try. Are you sure you haven't got something tucked away in a bottom drawer somewhere?'

'Quite sure. I don't waste time doodling. I work to order. Offer me a commission and I'd do my best to come up with something, but I couldn't guarantee that it'd be the instant hit you're hoping for.'

'What about your book?'

'Book?'

'Didn't Fran drag you away to talk to a journalist about a book you've illustrated?'

'Oh, right. I see where this is going.'

'No—' Something about the way she'd stiffened warned him that he'd made a mistake. But it was too late to do anything about it, and if she did have something... 'Didn't she?'

She drew back a little from the table. Inches. It felt like yards.

'I hate to disappoint you, but it's not what you're looking for. Thousands of children have not already fallen in love with my characters. Mothers are not forming a queue as we speak to beat a path to your door, hoping to snap them up for their little darlings.'

'Are you absolutely sure about that?'

'Down boy,' she said, laughing, but not altogether convincingly. 'I'm truly sorry, but it was just a one-off alphabet special I put together for Toby's birthday.'

'Oh, I see.' He'd offended her for nothing. 'I thought...' He wasn't sure what he'd thought. 'Did he like it?'

'Of course. All the pictures in the book are of his favourite things. I even scanned a photograph of him when I got to the letter T.'

'"T is for Toby"?' Somewhere at the back of his head a light went on. It was a very dim light, no more than fifteen watts, but there was *something*. 'He must have been thrilled with it.'

'He was. And when he took it to his playgroup all the other mothers begged Fran to get me to make them for their kids, too.'

'This was bad?' he asked, confused.

'No, but I did it for Toby. It wouldn't be the same if everyone else had one.'

'So what was the point of showing it to the journalist?'

'Oh, that was nothing to do with me. It's all on the computer, and Fran plagued me into letting her print off a dozen copies—using the "T is for telephone" that I'd drawn before I had the idea of using Toby's photograph.' She pulled a face. 'There's no stopping her since she launched herself into business. She's decided that if I won't make the effort, she's going to find me a publisher.'

He sensed something behind her words, something more that she wasn't saying, but he didn't press it.

'You don't think that's going to happen?'

She smiled, as if driving away demons. 'Let's just say that I have a better grasp than she does of how difficult it is to break into the illustrated book market.'

'What did the journalist have to say?'

'That she'll get back to me.'

There was an edge to her voice, a suggestion that she wouldn't be holding her breath, and he realised that the confidence she radiated was the thinnest of shells. It would be so very easy to hurt her. She was right to guard herself against his kind of carelessness.

Stick to business.

'Have you got a copy here?' he asked. 'I'd like to see for myself.'

She backed across the room, took a book from a cupboard containing art supplies and handed it to him. The illustrations had been printed on both sides of heavy, high-quality paper, and the covers were made of dark blue board held together with a bright red plastic comb binder. It might have been put together at home, but it looked and felt anything but home-made.

'It's not going to be any use to you,' she warned, as he flipped through the pages. 'Who's going to buy a birthday card featuring "B is for balloon"?'

The drawings were crisp, bright, appealing. They'd look wonderful on wrapping paper, he thought. But she was right. They wouldn't make particularly exciting cards.

'They're very colourful balloons,' he said.

'But not exactly personal.'

'It might appeal to someone who has an infant with a name beginning with the letter B,' he suggested, because he really wanted to be able to use them. That light at the back of his mind became a little brighter. Then, because she didn't seem particularly impressed, 'Or for someone who loves balloons.'

'Or who's "B for busy"?' she prompted.

'Is that a subtle hint that I've taken up enough of your time?'

'You thought that was subtle? Boy, you must have really thick skin.'

'I was simply being polite,' he assured her, with a grin.

'Is that a fact? And I thought we'd decided against that.'

'Sorry. Force of habit. I'll try not to do it again. But I am sorry that I can't use the illustrations.'

'Believe me, I'm disappointed to. The royalties from card sales would be very welcome. Meanwhile, I have a commission to finish if I'm going to eat next month.' She backed away from the table, turned, and tucked herself in beneath her drawing board. 'Thank you for lunch. I'm sorry you had a wasted journey.'

'It wasn't wasted,' he assured her. 'I've learned a lot. If I have any more bright ideas can I bring them over to have them shot down in flames?'

'I'm always happy to put a man in his place. Bring an avocado sandwich next time.'

'Avocado?'

'Avocado on wholemeal bread, with a squeeze of lemon juice and a sprinkle of freshly ground black pepper.'

Almost an invitation, he thought, making sure to keep his smile to himself as he looked over her shoulder at the picture she was working on. She was using pastels, and the mauves and purples of heather-clad hills were mirrored in the last of a sunset gleaming on a flat sea; in the distance a couple were silhouetted at the water's edge. It was quite different in style from the alphabet book.

It wasn't her first attempt. He bent and picked up one she'd discarded. There wasn't anything wrong with it—it was practically identical. But she'd drawn something on top of it. 'What's this?'

She turned to see what he was holding and came as close as she ever would to blushing.

'Nothing…'

He waited.

'I had this idea for a cartoon strip, that's all.'

'A superheroine in a wheelchair? Does she have a name?'

'Hattie Hot Wheels.' Then, 'Don't you dare laugh!'

'As if I would,' he said. It didn't take a psychologist to warn him that this was more than just a drawing, and he turned instead to the new picture on the drawing board. 'You're really very talented, Matty.'

She looked up, then quickly away again. 'No, you can't have it, Sebastian. It's a commission. An illustration for a magazine story.'

'I don't want it,' he assured her. 'But you've caught the melancholy feel of a late summer evening very well.' Or maybe it wasn't the picture at all, but something in her eyes that made him think that the story was about an ending, not a beginning.

'It isn't finished,' she said, leaving him with the distinct impression that he'd touched something raw. 'Now, if there's nothing else?' There was no mistaking the message. Go. Now.

'I'm sorry. I've already taken up too much of your time. Can I take this with me?'

He held up the alphabet book.

'Be my guest,' she said, without turning around, reaching for a stick of pastel. 'Just be sure to show it to any publishers or journalists you happen to meet, or you'll have to answer to Fran.'

'I'll do that if you'll promise to have lunch with me next time I ask.'

'You don't give up, do you, Sebastian?' she asked, looking back at him.

He could have told her that patient persistence was the one trait he and his family had in common.

The Earl might have little patience for business, but he was happy to stand for hours up to his thighs in cold water, teasing some wily old trout out of its hiding place, only to let it go again once he'd proved that he was the smarter of the two.

His sisters, typically lazy teenagers for the most part, had applied the same passion to grooming their mounts to glossy perfection before a gymkhana for no more reward than a rosette for Best Turned-out Horse and Rider.

But he said nothing, and after a moment she waved him away with the stick of pastel.

'I was joking about the publishers. Take the book.' And then she looked back at the painting. 'No strings attached.'

Matty remained, hand poised over the picture, until she heard the front door close. Then she leaned back, her hand shaking so much that she dropped the pastel. It didn't matter. She'd lied. The picture was finished. Sebastian was right; it did have that aching, last time, end-of-the-summer feel to it. But then she'd done it from memory.

CHAPTER FOUR

SEBASTIAN ignored the cruising black cabs and walked to the office, giving the light in his head time to grow a little brighter. By the time he'd reached his office it was almost bright enough to read by.

'Blanche, I think I've got it,' he said, as she followed him, clutching a bundle of messages. He waved them away. 'Take a look at this.'

She flipped through the book, smiling at the pictures. Then looked up, slightly puzzled. 'They're charming drawings, but I don't see how we can use them.'

'Not as they are,' he said, settling into George's huge leather chair. 'But suppose we produced a series of cards with actual names on them? The balloon card for instance, with, say, "B is for…"' He gestured, encouraging her to come up with a name.

'Bonnie?' she offered. 'Or Bertie. Or Brad.' There was something about the way she said them that suggested she wasn't exactly overwhelmed with enthusiasm.

'You're not sold on the idea?'

'There's nothing wrong with the *idea*,' she said, carefully stressing the word 'idea'. 'The simple ideas are usually the best.'

'But?'

'But I was simply wondering about the logistics.'

'Logistics?'

'How many names do you think there are?'

'Well, hundreds. Thousands. But obviously we'd just use the most popular ones. The way they do for mugs and

60

keyrings and those painted china door plaques that you see in motorway service stations. There is an annual list of the most popular children's names, isn't there?'

'I believe so.'

'But?' he repeated.

She sank into the chair opposite. 'I'm not saying it's impossible, Sebastian, but you have to look at it from the retailer's point of view. With just one name of each letter for boys and girls you have fifty-two cards.' Then, pre-empting him, 'Okay, forgetting X—although I'm sure there are some of those and it must be jolly hard to always be ignored—fifty cards. That's a big investment in a single range. And only one card would be right for each customer. If there were no ''Peter'' cards left, then ''Paul'' wouldn't do. Your customer would go somewhere else.'

'Those logistics will get you every time,' he said, swinging round to stare out of the window. 'Damn. I really thought I had something.'

He swept his a hand through his hair and immediately remembered Matty doing the same thing, the way her hair had stood up in a little quiff that he'd wanted to smooth down.

'I thought I'd have more time to find my way around before I had to make these kind of decisions,' he said.

'Yes, well, while you were out I made some phone calls. Spoke to one or two people we've published in the past. I'm waiting for them to get back to me.'

He took a deep breath, swung back to face her.

'Thank you, Blanche. I suspect that without you this company would have disappeared a long time ago.'

'Very possibly. But it's a bit of a long shot. Best save the congratulations for the moment.' Then, firmly changing the subject by picking up the alphabet book, 'This kind of leap-off-the-page quality is rare.'

A description that fitted both the artist and her work. He doubted Matty would have missed the obvious, the way he had. She certainly wouldn't have been as tactful as Blanche, but he had no doubt that, while laughing at him, she'd have made him smile, too.

'Matty is something of a one-off, too,' he said.

'Maybe you should consider offering her a commission?' Blanche prompted. 'Get her under contract before someone else finds her.'

'You may have a point, but I doubt that I'd be the best person to negotiate with her. For some reason she refuses to take me seriously.'

'You mean she's smart, as well as talented?' she asked. Then her cheeks flamed with embarrassment. 'I'm sorry. That came out all wrong.'

'Did it?' he asked, before taking pity on her. 'Not that wrong, Blanche.'

One of her shoulders lifted in an awkward little shrug. 'George used to talk about you sometimes.'

'Nothing good, obviously.'

'It wasn't like that. He was very fond of you. But he worried about you, too. He said that you'd cut yourself off from everything but work. That by the time you woke up and realised what you'd been missing it would be too late.'

'No one could ever accuse him of doing that.'

'No.'

'So was he happy?'

'Sometimes. For a little while. But he never stopped looking, hoping.' She looked away, staring at a pigeon that had settled on the window ledge.

'Maybe he should have taken his eyes off the horizon

for a moment and looked closer to home,' he said, thinking of all the glamorous, shallow women his cousin had lavished time and money on, with little in return but to be seen with a lovely woman on his arm. They'd had that in common, except that, unlike George, he'd learned to keep a tight hold on his heart. Then, more briskly, 'Getting back to Miss Lang, why don't you give her a call? Tell her you've just been appointed as...' He paused to consider what title to bestow on her. 'Acquisitions Co-ordinator for Coronet Cards.'

Surprised out of the threatening tears, she said, 'Acquisitions Co-ordinator?'

'If you don't like it, you can think up your own title. We'll sort out an appropriate salary later.'

'Oh, no, really...' Then, 'Are you sure?'

'Don't undersell yourself, Blanche. You know more about this business than anyone, and, since I'm going to be leaning on you pretty heavily, you should be properly rewarded.'

She thought about it for a moment, then, apparently convinced, said, 'So what do you want me to talk to Miss Lang about?'

'First,' he said, fingers resting lightly on the alphabet book, 'I want these designs under option before some bright publisher decides to buy the book.'

'How long an option?'

'Six months.' There was no use tying them up for longer. If they hadn't used them in six months they never would, and after that they'd revert to Matty, leaving her free to sell to someone else. 'I'll leave you to negotiate a reasonable fee.'

Was that completely selfish of him?

Would a publisher, be he ever so interested, even look at the book once she'd parted with valuable rights? But then she'd told him herself that the chances of finding a publisher were slim. Besides, if she didn't want to sell him an option nothing on earth would persuade her.

'What else?'

He looked at Blanche, not sure what she was talking about.

'You said that was the first thing you wanted. It implies you want more.'

'Yes, I suppose it does. There's nothing specific. Talk to her about the market. See if she comes up with any ideas, and if she does offer her a commission to produce the artwork.'

'You don't want much, then,' she said wryly.

'Nothing you can't handle, I'm sure. But if you decide to take her out to lunch, clear the choice of restaurant with her first.'

'Let's see how far we get on the telephone, first, shall we? I assume you do have her number?'

He'd seen it on the phone in Matty's kitchen when he'd fetched water for the Scotch at the wedding party. He hadn't deliberately memorised it; he just had that kind of brain. 'Call her this afternoon,' he said, writing it down on a sticky note before peeling it off and handing it to her.

'I'll get right on to it.' Then, as he propelled himself out of the chair and headed for the door, she said, 'Where are you going?'

'Don't look so worried, Blanche,' he said. 'I'm not going to run off and leave you holding the baby. It occurs to me that I should do a little basic research. Check out the competition, walk the stores, talk to the retailers. Get a feel for the business. By the time you have something for me to look at, I might have some idea what I'm doing.'

'Right,' she said. 'In the meantime, what do you want me to do about these messages?'

He took them from her, flicking through them. 'File, file, file,' he said, tossing the three from journalists straight into the bin. 'Call the rest back and make appointments. But not until next week if at all possible.'

'And when will you be back? In case Miss Lang asks.'

'She won't.'

For the past week he had been paralysed by anger at the way the heady upward spiral of his career had been brought to a juddering halt. At having his very satisfactory life yanked out from under him.

Had Matty felt that way after the accident? He couldn't begin to imagine how her life had changed. Permanently. How she'd had to relearn how to do even the simplest of tasks, things that she'd once taken for granted. What she'd lost.

He'd lost nothing. In six months his life would still be waiting for him to pick it up. If not exactly where he'd left it, then not far off.

Hardly surprising she wasn't prepared to give him the time of day when he was behaving like a spoilt brat about it.

Right now he needed to stop feeling sorry for himself, get his act together and do everything he could to turn Coronet into a company that the major players would be fighting to buy. And half a year at the sharp end could only improve his understanding of what his clients went through. Make him better at his job.

Which was all he cared about.

'For me, then,' Blanche said, breaking into his thoughts. 'I'd like to know when you'll be back in the office.'

'Thursday morning,' he said briskly. 'You can hold the fort until then, can't you?'

'It wouldn't be the first time,' Blanche replied. But softly.

Matty jumped at the sound of the phone. It wouldn't be him. She didn't want it to be him...

She hated this breathless expectation, recognising the danger, the treacherous heart-lift that came with the anticipation of a longed-for voice, the reckless abandonment of all prospect of joy to another's hands.

She'd surrendered her right to that self-indulgence. Those feelings were for other people. She counted the rings until the answering machine picked up.

Two...three...four...five...

She grabbed it before the sixth ring, holding the receiver hard against her jackhammer heart while she took a slow breath. Only then did she lift it to her ear and speak.

'Matty Lang.'

Her voice was cool, detached, betrayed nothing. A lesson hard learned...

'Miss Lang, my name is Blanche Appleby. I'm the, um, Acquisitions Co-ordinator for Coronet Cards...'

It wasn't him. Her heart slowed achingly, painfully, to something nearer a normal beat as she tried to untangle the mixture of disappointment and relief that swept over her.

'Miss Lang? Are you there?'

'Sorry, yes...'

'I hope this isn't an inconvenient moment, but I'd like to talk to you about Coronet buying a six-month option on your alphabet illustrations.'

Coronet Cards? Sebastian wanted her drawings and he'd asked someone else to call and make her an offer?

The confusion of feelings polarised, bringing disappointment into sharper focus...

She swallowed. What had she expected? This was business. He wanted her illustrations and the food, wine, had been his way of wooing them from her. And now he had them. So why would he waste any more time tying up the loose ends?

But he'd said he'd come to see her because she made him laugh...

Oh, get real, Matty, she told herself firmly. He knew all along that you had something that might be useful to him. He was smart enough to make it seem like an afterthought, that was all.

Big-shot bankers did that all the time. Probably.

'Miss Lang?' Once again the woman had to prompt a response from her.

'I'm so sorry. I was ...' away with the fairies, the *Forest Fairies* '...distracted by someone for just a moment. I'm all yours now.'

'I said I thought it might be helpful if we could meet to discuss the details. Would it be convenient for you to come to the office?'

Blanche Appleby was not as smooth an operator as Sebastian Wolseley. He wouldn't have asked an open question, given her the opportunity to say a flat no. He'd have offered two alternatives, pushing her to choose between them.

When she was slow to answer, the woman tried again.

'Or we could meet over lunch somewhere, if you'd prefer. Wherever is convenient for you.'

Lunch. What was it with this company? Did they think

all it took was a sliver of smoked salmon and a glass of wine to get a signature on a contract?

Because, as yet, nothing was signed.

'Actually, Ms Appleby—'

'Blanche, please.'

'Blanche,' she repeated. 'I'm not interested in selling an option. Perhaps Sebastian didn't mention that I'm actively seeking a publisher for the book?'

It was pride talking, of course. The most stupid cutting-off-your-nose-to-spite-your-face kind of pride.

Sebastian Wolseley was willing to pay her good money simply to have first dibs on her illustrations for the next six months.

There wasn't an illustrator in the country who didn't have an alphabet book going the rounds of the publishers, and most of them would have jumped at such an offer.

Okay, it wouldn't be a fortune, and there was no guarantee that they would ever be used, but it was found money—money she hadn't had to work for—and it could go straight into her 'country cottage' fund. And in six months they'd be hers again—in the unlikely event that a publisher ever was interested in the whole package.

Too late now to think of that. 'If that's all?' she prompted.

'No!' Blanche, sounding flustered, rushed on. 'Sebastian wanted me to talk to you about the market in general. He is really taken with your work. He came back to the office full of plans for an alphabet series. Nothing usable, unfortunately...'

Not usable? So why on earth would he want an option?

'...but he did authorise me to offer you a commission for artwork for any interesting ideas that you might have.'

'And that's what you want to talk about?'

'Yes,' she said, clearly relieved.

Well, that was different. Maybe she was being a little harsh. She had pretty much thrown him out. Maybe that was why he'd sent a deputy. A demonstration that he meant business.

Maybe it was time she stopped daydreaming and became a little more businesslike, too.

'Is he there?' she asked. 'I'd like a word.'

'I'm afraid not. He won't be in the office until Thursday.'

Oh, right. He was taking this *really* seriously.

'You'd be doing me a great personal favour if you'd at least consider the option, Miss Lang,' Blanche said. 'This is a promotion for me, and when Sebastian goes back to the States he'll need someone to run the company and...' She stopped, but the message was clear.

'And you want the job?'

Blanche Appleby hadn't a clue what was going on, Matty realised. Sebastian had given her a fancy title and she thought she had a chance to prove herself, when the truth was that, whether things were turned around sufficiently to find a buyer or whether they weren't, she was going to be dumped on life's scrap heap. What a bastard.

But then her taste in men had always been skin-deep. Just as long as they pleased her artist's eye...

'I've been doing it pretty much single-handed for the last three years,' Blanche said. 'Everything but make the final choice on artwork. And to be frank, George...George Wolseley...who founded the company...'

'Sebastian told me about him,' she said, rescuing her when Blanche Appleby appeared to choke up. 'You worked for him for a long time?'

'I was the first person he took on,' she said. 'The ink was scarcely dry on my Pitman's certificate. He was very dashing. Very handsome.'

It ran in the family. George Wolseley had obviously stolen his young secretary's heart and never given it back.

A warning if ever there was one.

'He had a triple bypass a while back, and he made a good recovery, considering, but he was never quite on top of things afterwards. He should probably have retired, taken it easier, but he really enjoyed coming into the office.'

To be cosseted by Blanche, no doubt, who was rattling on, saying far too much in her desperation to hang on to something precious to her.

'If I can just prove to Sebastian that I can handle the artwork, find new designs,' she went on, 'he'll have to give me a chance, won't he? At my age I'm never going to get another one.'

'Blanche—'

'Oh, who am I kidding? He's going to want someone younger. Forget chances. I'll be lucky if I ever get another—'

'Blanche!'

She stopped abruptly. Then, with a gasp of embarrassment, 'Oh, good grief, I'm so sorry. I don't know what came over me.'

'Blanche, it's okay—really.' And, having finally put a stop to the desperate flow, Matty said again, 'It's okay. You can have the option.' She wasn't doing it for Sebastian, or even for herself, but for another woman who'd had a rotten deal. If she couldn't help her any other way, she'd do what she could to make the company saleable, so that she didn't lose everything. 'You can have the option on the alphabet illustrations and I'll be happy to talk to you.'

*   *   *

'They're all the same, aren't they?'

Sebastian glanced at the woman standing next to him, middle-aged, harassed, searching through the extra-large novelty cards in her lunch break.

She nodded at the selection of children's birthday cards he was holding. 'I make all my own these days.'

'You do?'

He was assailed by a memory of his sisters battling with glue, felt and glitter one Christmas, before she said, 'On the computer.'

'Oh, right.' He'd known, in theory, that it was possible to produce your own greetings cards if you had the right software—Matty, after all, had produced an entire book on hers—but it simply hadn't occurred to him that anyone would bother. 'Is that cheaper? By the time you've bought card and envelopes, paid for the ink and what have you?'

'No, but that's not the point, is it? You can make them really individual. Even use your own photographs if you've got a decent printer.'

'I hadn't even thought about that,' he said, quite truthfully. Then, since she was, after all, in a card shop buying a greeting card, 'So what went wrong today?' He indicated the giant-sized card she'd picked up.

'This?' She looked at it without enthusiasm. 'I'm only buying this because one of the girls is leaving today and we need something really big for us all to sign.' She nodded in the direction of his own selection and said, 'Think about it.'

'I will. Thank you,' he called after her as she headed for the cash desk. Then, to himself, 'I will.'

It had been his intention to introduce himself to the manager, talk about the top-selling lines, ask her what she felt was missing from the cards on sale. But he replaced the cards and walked out into the bustle of the small shopping mall.

He'd spent Tuesday afternoon and most of Wednesday talking to the retailers and, apart from a fast-growing collection of top sellers—all of them produced by the competition—he'd learned nothing useful beyond the fact that the public had an apparently insatiable appetite for teddy bears and hedgehogs on their greetings cards, no matter what their age.

It had taken a chance remark to show him that anyone with access to a computer could do what he'd wanted to do: make a personalised card with a child's name on it. In fact they had one huge advantage over him and could use any name they wanted, no matter how unusual or quirky the spelling.

Which was when the lightbulb, still flickering dimly in the unfrequented back corridors of his brain, lit up like a lighthouse in a 'eureka' moment. And there was just one person he wanted to share it with.

Ignoring the 'Residents Only' parking restriction, he pulled up outside Matty's flat an hour later, clattered down the basement steps and rang the doorbell.

'Who is that?'

The voice coming through the speaker had a fractured, completely over-the-top foreign accent. Well, she'd warned him and, grinning at having caught her out, he said, 'Matty, it's Sebastian.'

There was a slight pause before the voice replied, 'Matty not here.'

Oh, right. Like he'd believe that.

'Very funny. Now, stop messing about and let me in,' he said. 'I've got something important to tell you.'

'I tell *you*,' the same disembodied voice enunciated slowly and clearly, 'Ma-ttee no-ot he-errre.'

Then the speaker went dead.

He pressed the bell a couple of times. Knocked. Called out to her. 'Matty! Don't do this. I've had this absolutely brilliant idea for how we can use your illustrations.'

The speaker crackled again and the same voice said, 'Go away.'

'Okay, babe. You're busy. I get the message. Call me when you have a moment.'

He backed slowly up the steps, expecting that any moment she would relent and buzz him in. Only when he reached pavement level did he accept that it wasn't going to happen and turn away—just in time to see a traffic warden tuck a parking notice under his windscreen wiper.

'I'm sorry,' she said defensively, taking a step back, 'but this is a Residents Only parking area.'

'No need to apologise,' he replied, plucking the penalty notice from beneath the wiper. 'I'm the one illegally parked. You're just doing your job.'

That earned him a smile, but, sweet though it was, it wasn't the one he'd been hoping for. Since that was denied him, he might as well go back to the office and see if Blanche had done any better with Matty. Before he gave her a chance to poke holes in his latest brainwave, however, he'd talk to someone who could tell him if what he had in mind was actually possible.

He tossed the parking ticket into the glove compartment, took out his cellphone and called up a number in the memory.

The parking warden shook her head, indicating with a broad gesture that he should move on. But she'd already given him a ticket. Short of calling up the clampers she was out of options. And, having done her duty, she moved on, still smiling.

*   *   *

'These have come up a treat,' Matty said, looking at the mock-ups the production department had made of the botanical prints.

'I suppose that's the difference between us,' said Blanche. 'I saw shabby; you saw antique. Printed on matching card, they look really expensive.'

'Do you do wrapping paper?'

'Yes, but… What?'

'I was thinking that if you could have the image blown up to standard wrapping paper size…' Matty shook her head. 'No, it'll be too much of stretch. They'll pixelate. I'll have to think about that. But there's no reason why you shouldn't offer prints, is there? Most card shops do gifts, and having the birthday card and gift tag to match the gift might appeal. Worth trying out on the big buyer…'

At which point she realised that Blanche was no longer paying attention, but looking beyond her to the door.

CHAPTER FIVE

SEBASTIAN had been standing in the open doorway for a full minute before either woman noticed him, so absorbed were they in what they were doing.

A full minute of grace in which to watch Matty do that thing where she pushed her fingers through her hair, leaving it standing up in an untidy little ruff of curls as she concentrated on the prints spread out in front of her.

A minute to watch her forehead pucker in a thoughtful frown, smooth again as an idea pleased her, and to feel good that she was here, on his territory.

To acknowledge another emotion, too: something darker, almost akin to jealousy that she had responded to Blanche's appeal when his own had fallen on apparently deaf ears.

Ridiculous.

He didn't do jealous. You had to be emotionally engaged to indulge in such pointless, time-wasting postures.

You had to care, have access to the kind of feelings that had been burned from his psyche years ago.

But she looked so perfectly at home. So in control.

The gleam of gold gypsy hoops in her ears, a full, softly draped amber silk shirt that he knew would perfectly match her eyes, drew attention to her upper body. Her strong shoulders, long, lithe arms. Her legs were encased in drab green moleskin jeans; her boots were soft, dark chocolate suede. If they had been chosen, as he assumed, not to catch the eye, then it was a strategy that had failed.

How could he have ever thought she was ordinary? Nondescript?

Power, strength, radiated from her.

He didn't move, didn't make a sound, but she suddenly swivelled round as if conscious, on some primitive level, of his presence. And he had one more moment of grace when her face was entirely his before she retreated behind a mask, a warm, bright, protective force field, which until then he hadn't begun to suspect she habitually wore.

A moment to fool himself that she was as glad to see him as he was to find her there.

'Sebastian. I thought you were away until tomorrow.'

Was that why she had come? Because she'd been sure he wouldn't be there? She was deliberately avoiding him?

Intrigued, rather than offended, he said, 'Hello, Matty.'

He'd kissed her cousin's cheek without thought when he'd met her in Matty's flat. As casual and meaningless a gesture as shaking a man's hand. Halfway across the office, he discovered that casual and meaningless had no place in his relationship with Matty, and instead he picked up one of the mock-ups.

'Has Blanche taken you on as a consultant?' he asked, as casually as he knew how.

Matty wasn't the only one who knew how to protect herself.

'Yes,' Blanche intervened quickly, before she could deny it. Matty, mouth open to deny it, found herself caught between exposing Blanche and colluding in the lie. 'At least I've made the offer. I'm going to need a little help twisting Matty's arm.'

'It will be my pleasure,' he said, looking directly at her. 'These are very classy.' Like the woman, he thought. 'I like your print idea, too, Matty.'

'Thank you.'

He hadn't taken his eyes off her, and now she lifted her head and returned the look. Direct, challenging. It was not a comfortable exchange. He had the distinct impression that she was angry with him, but couldn't for the life of him imagine why.

He raised his brows a millimetre in silent query and, not breaking eye contact with Matty, said, 'Why don't you go and organise some frame samples, Blanche? Sort out the costing.'

On the point of saying something, Blanche had second thoughts. 'I'll get right onto it,' she said, closing the door behind her as she left the office.

Still holding Matty's gaze, he turned the card over, so that the front was facing her. 'I thought these prints were nothing but junk when I looked at them.'

'Did you?' The words were little more than a squeak, and she cleared her throat, blinked, then looked at the card, rather than him, suggesting that whatever problem she had with him, she didn't want to confront it. 'They were just a bit foxed. I scanned them and cleaned them up on your computer.'

'Well, they look great now.'

On safer ground, she relaxed a little. 'The trick is not to overdo it. I didn't want to lose the suggestion of age, just the shabbiness.'

'Well, good job.' Realising that Matty was being forced to look up at him, he pulled up a chair, sat down alongside her and then leaned closer, so that their shoulders were all but touching, before he said, 'Have I done something to upset or annoy you, Matty?'

Matty felt something akin to an electric shock as Sebastian's shoulder brushed against hers.

'Me?'

Oh, good grief, her voice was squeaking again. She'd known from the start that it was a mistake to glare at him like that, but he wasn't supposed to be in the office today. Blanche had been quite certain about that.

'What makes you think I'm annoyed?' He didn't answer. 'What could you possibly do that would have the slightest effect on me?' she asked, filling the uncomfortable silence.

Apart from being here.

'I don't know, Matty. Your glare was eloquent, but non-specific. I thought we were friends.'

'Did you? And what about Blanche? Is she your friend, too?'

'This is about Blanche?'

'You promoted her, Sebastian. She's over the moon. Thrilled to finally have a chance to prove herself. But it's all a lie. You're going to take that away from her in a few months and put her out to grass—'

'I didn't—don't—have to do anything,' he reminded her.

'Yes, you do!' She lifted a hand, acknowledging that she was being unreasonable. 'Did you know that she was in love with George? For years.'

'Did she tell you that?'

'Blanche? Of course not. But it shines out of her. You can hear it in her voice, in everything she says about him. All the while he was off chasing pretty little trophy bimbos she was here, loving him. Even when he was sick he still couldn't see it. Had to have some dewy little creature with sticky fingers to pander to him.'

'His weakness. His misfortune.'

'No, Sebastian. Hers. He must have known. Men always know. He used her, and now you're doing the same.'

'At least I'm recognising her abilities, even if it's too late to mean very much. Would you rather I just walked away?'

'I would rather you were honest with her. Tell her the truth.'

'I shouldn't have told you.'

'No, you shouldn't. It's her future you're gambling

with, not mine.' Then, because she knew he was doing what he thought right, she let it go. 'Oh, look, take no notice of me. What do I know? I'm sure you're doing what you think is best.'

'If ever a man was damned with faint praise...' he said, but he was, amazingly, smiling at her.

'What?' she demanded. He did that thing with his eyebrows again. 'You've got something, haven't you? That's why you came back early. Tell me!'

'Before I tell Blanche?' he asked. 'Would that be fair?'

'Probably not,' she admitted, irritated to discover that she was smiling, too.

He flipped the card he was holding over and said, 'You could use these botanical prints for packs of notelets, don't you think?'

Teasing her.

'I think you've been paying attention in class,' Matty said. Then, 'I also think that you're dying to tell me about the idea you have.'

'I'd certainly welcome your opinion,' he said, tossing the card onto a nearby table. 'Blanche told you what I've been doing?'

'She mentioned you were doing a little research.' She forced herself to sound bored. 'Fairly basic practice with any new venture, I'd have thought.'

'It's really opened my eyes to the potential. I discovered that our largest buyer has nearly eight hundred outlets, for instance.'

'That's an awful lot of cards.'

'It's not just cards, though, is it? Using designs like this we could produce notebooks, address books, even gift packs with *pot pourri*, or essential oils...'

'Both,' she assured him. 'And if this is your big idea I have to tell you that Blanche is already on it. We've even got a name for the collection. Botanicals.' She lifted her hands in a 'job done' gesture. 'It's simple, memorable—does what it says on the—'

'I'm sold,' Sebastian replied, taking the hand nearest to him, grasping it warmly, as if they were a team. 'Botanicals it is.'

It took all her concentration not to fall into that trap. There were no teams here. Despite her attack on him, she was no better. Everyone at Coronet was working for their own selfish ends.

'Right,' she said. 'Job done. Blanche can handle the rest.'

'That job,' he agreed. 'But what about the three- to six-year-olds?' Sebastian asked, as Matty reclaimed her hand without fuss. He fought the urge to tighten his grip. Hold on. 'Any progress there?'

'Nothing yet, but I'm thinking about it. In fact I'd better get back to the drawing board.' Suiting the action to her words, she moved her chair in the direction of the door.

'I called at your flat,' he said. 'Before I came back to the office.'

'Did you?' she asked, and the fact that she stopped, swivelled her chair to face him, suggested that she was finding it almost as difficult to leave as he was to let her go. 'Why?'

'Because I wanted to talk to you. All I got for my pains was a flea in my ear from some mad woman who kept saying "Ma-ttee no-ot heerrrre".' He rolled his r's dramatically and she laughed.

'Connie isn't mad. She's Greek. She's Fran's "rescue" housekeeper.'

'I've heard of rescue dogs—but housekeepers?'

'She was abandoned by a man who treated her as little better than slave labour. Fran brought her home when she collapsed from hunger in the park.'

'That's definitely a rescue. Your cousin sounds like a very special woman.'

'She is, but she'd probably tell you that she got the best of the bargain. Connie has a heart as big as a house, and she's wonderful with the children. She was wonderful with me, too. But then we had the ''rescue'' thing in common.'

She held his gaze, as if defying him to suggest she hadn't needed rescuing. Or perhaps simply confronting him with the reality of her life, reminding him that holding hands with her was not a simple thing.

'Fran took you in after the accident?'

'As soon as I'd been through rehab. She made it sound as if I was doing her a favour, making her get to grips with the basement. Clearing out the junk, extending it, turning it into a proper garden flat.'

'It must have increased the value of the property,' he pointed out.

'Not with me as sitting tenant.' Then, 'And Connie still acts as if I can't do my own housework. The minute I leave the flat, she's down there with the vacuum.'

'She was certainly down there half an hour ago,' he assured her. 'Whether or not she was vacuuming, I couldn't say.'

She gave a little shrug, as if to say that it didn't matter one way or the other. Then she grinned broadly and said, 'You thought it was me, didn't you?'

He neither confirmed nor denied it.

'You did!'

She laughed out loud, delighted to have caught him out.

'I'm glad you think it's funny,' he said, then, fairly sure that it would provide her with further amusement, added, 'While under the mistaken impression that it was you, I spent rather too long attempting to persuade her to let me in and got a parking ticket.'

He was not disappointed.

'Oh, dear. Poor Sebastian,' she said. 'You have had a rough morning.'

'Not at all.' And he finally stopped teasing her and explained why it had been anything but a rough morning.

On the contrary. And, now he was looking at her, it had, if anything, improved.

Matty wished she hadn't been so precipitate. She could, if she'd been braver, have been sitting beside Sebastian right now, her hand in his, as he explained his idea for print-on-demand cards, available at the point of sale, instead of a clear three feet away.

Not that she was finding it particularly easy to concentrate, let alone drop in the odd question to show that she was paying attention, even from this safe distance. Simply looking at him made thinking difficult.

Her mind would keep taking off on little 'wonder' adventures.

Wondering how his hair would feel against her fingers if she pushed back the cowlick that was feathering his forehead...

Wondering how his skin would smell, fresh from the shower, how it would taste...

Wondering how it would feel to have his long fingers stroking her...

The sheer effort of dragging herself back to reality made her shudder, and Sebastian stopped talking about software programs and computer hardware and said, 'Matty? Are you okay?'

She swallowed, nodded. 'Sorry. It's the air-conditioning,' she lied.

Her only problem with the temperature was inside. And it was heat not cold that was giving her a hard time. That, and hard common sense loudly repeating over and over, *This is insanity. Stop this. Stop this now...*

But when she'd turned and seen him standing there, in the doorway, her heart had been seized by an emotion beyond her power to still.

She was so used to playing the flirt and getting away with it completely unscathed that it had never occurred to her what risks she might be running when she'd reached out to him, breaking into his dark reverie at Fran and Guy's reception.

The patronising men who thought they were doing her a favour simply by talking to her were such an easy target, practically falling over their own feet in their rush to escape when they realised that they'd strayed into quicksand.

And while the decent men stayed to chat, flirted back, occasionally became friends and might have become more given encouragement, she'd never been touched. Had thought she was safe, beyond reach...

'Won't it be expensive to set up and maintain?' she asked, forcing herself to concentrate on the idea rather than the man voicing it. Reality rather than fantasy. 'What about staff training?'

'I'm assured that it should be no more of a problem than a simple photocopier. But you can see for yourself as soon as the prototype is ready.'

'You've already organised it?'

'I have a brother-in-law who's in the business.'

'Really? Sisters are useful for something, then?'

'I wouldn't go that far. Anyway, according to him, there's hardware available that can do this with a little tweaking. All we need is someone to put the software together—he knows the very man, apparently—and we're in business.' She must have looked doubtful, because he said, 'It's not exactly new technology, Matty. You can print yourself personalised business cards at any motorway service area.'

'Yes, but—'

'This isn't so very different. The designs are fixed; it's just the individual names that are programmed in by the buyer. There is one small problem.'

'Really? Just one?'

'I not only need your drawings, I'm going to have to ask you to adapt them slightly.'

'And if I won't?'

'Well, there are other alphabet books.' His expression was deadpan, but his eyes, the colour of the sea on a good day, assured her that he knew she wouldn't let him down. 'I'm sure there are any number of publishers out there who'd be happy to take my money.'

'True. Maybe you should ask your consultant what she'd advise,' she suggested.

'Good plan. As my consultant, what would you advise, Matty?'

'I'd advise you to save your money and use the option you've already paid for.'

'You agree?' He reached across, and this time when he took her hand she had no plans to pull away. 'Thank you.'

'Thank Blanche. She had a cheque waiting for me yesterday morning. I'm assuming it won't bounce.'

'You have my personal guarantee.' Then, tightening his grip on her hand, 'You really are cold. Maybe we should continue this discussion somewhere warmer. Are you hungry?'

'Are you making it your life's work to feed me?' Then, because a life's work suggested for ever, 'No, don't answer that. Actually, I'm starving.' And, because he was not the only one who could tease, she added, 'Will you be able to get a table at Giovanni's at such short notice?'

'You'd be surprised what I can do, but I had something a little less formal in mind. I think we should take advantage of the sun and eat *al fresco*.'

'A picnic in the park?' Then, because she knew it was not sensible—and if she was nothing else she was sensible—she said, 'Pity. Blanche is sending out for something. Another time, perhaps.'

'Oh, no. I'm the boss. I get first dibs on your company.'

'But she's already—'

'She can share with someone else.'

'All right. But doesn't a picnic require food?'

'You think I'd call on a lady at lunchtime empty-handed? I'll have you know that I arrived at your flat fully armed with an avocado sandwich, exactly as ordered.' He indicated something on the table behind her. She looked back over her shoulder and saw one of those brown paper carriers from the expensive bakery. He must have put it down when he arrived, she realised.

Just how long had he been standing there before she'd felt the warning prickle at the back of her neck?

'I was joking about that,' she said. 'Oh, Lord, now I'm totally embarrassed.'

'Since it means you can't possibly turn me down, I forgive you.'

'Can't I? Should you be taking time out to indulge yourself in this way? Shouldn't you be working on your master plan to save Coronet?' she asked, grabbing the first excuse that came to mind.

'You are my master plan,' he said.

That was good. She was perfectly happy to be his master plan. It was holding hands and picnics in the park that were problematic.

She finally found the strength of mind to remove her hand from his and said, 'All the more reason for me to get back to my drawing board and start work adapting the drawings for you.'

'This will be a working lunch,' he assured her. 'First we have to negotiate a fee for all this extra work you're going to have to do. Then we need to discuss the rest of the alphabet range. I was wondering if you'd done anything else for Toby? I've got some ideas, but—'

'You're planning a whole range of alphabet goods?'

'Oh, *now* you're interested,' he said, with a grin. 'You certainly know how to deflate a man's ego.'

'What's your ego got to do with it?' she asked. 'As Coronet's consultant, it's my duty to make the most of the company's investment. As the designer of this proposed new range, I have to look after mine.'

'So that's yes on both counts, then?'

'Yes,' she said, rather ungraciously, considering that she'd just talked herself into it. 'And, yes. But it had better be a damn fine sandwich.'

'If it isn't,' he said, 'I'll take you to the bakery so that you can complain in person. Now, shall we go?'

Sebastian strolled alongside Matty as they crossed the road and entered the park, keeping an eye on the traffic, flinching as skateboarders flew past in front of her. She seemed totally oblivious to the lack of care people took around her; presumably she was used to it.

While he was ready to shout at some careless oaf who thought his rollerblades gave him right of way, she simply adjusted her speed to avoid a collision and then moved on as if nothing had happened.

'That's better,' she said, as she parked her chair beside a shady bench ignored by the sun-worshipping office workers who'd chosen to stretch out on the grass.

'What?' he asked, as he sat alongside her.

'You've stopped twitching.'

'I do not twitch.'

Her only response was a grin.

'Okay, maybe I was a little anxious, but the pedestrian

public doesn't exactly go out of its way to make space for you, does it?'

'Why should it?'

'Well—' It occurred to him, belatedly, that his best course of action at this point would be to change the subject. 'No reason.' Then, because, genuinely outraged, he couldn't hold back his anger, 'But that boy on rollerblades missed you by inches.'

'That's enough.'

Whether she was referring to the inches or to the entire subject he had no way of knowing, and he played safe by agreeing with her.

'I suppose it is.'

'Or perhaps you think I should carry a bell to warn other road users to clear a path?'

Now he knew he was really in trouble.

'I have no thoughts. I am,' he admitted, 'utterly thoughtless.'

At least she smiled at that. 'Shall we change the subject now?' she offered.

'I'd like that. But only if you think I've suffered enough.'

'You're a man. There isn't enough suffering in the entire world,' she assured him, but kindly. 'However, this is supposed to be a business lunch.'

'So it is.' Taking advantage of the fact that she'd just taken a bite out of her sandwich and was in no position to say anything, he added, 'Unfortunately I lied about the "business" part of it.'

Her mouth might have been occupied, but her eyes were eloquent.

'Did the sandwich meet with your approval?' he risked a little while later, as she brushed the crumbs from her lap for the sparrows who'd been hovering expectantly.

'Thank you. It was delicious. I could definitely get used to having you around.'

'Have you had enough? There's a spare—cheese and pickle? Or would you rather move on to pudding?'

'Pudding?' As she leaned across to peek in the carrier and see what he'd bought one of her wayward curls brushed against his cheek and he felt every skin cell tighten, shockingly, in response to her closeness. 'What pudding?' she demanded, looking up, her eyes more black than amber in the shadowy light beneath the trees. As if aware of having stepped over some invisible line, she said, 'There's, um, not so much as an apple in here.'

'Am I never to be given the benefit of the doubt?' he asked, capturing her face as, just a little flustered, she began to back off. Lifting her chin so that she was forced to keep looking at him. 'When will you begin to trust me, Matty?'

'I…um…' she began, then stopped, for once short of a snappy answer. Lost, it seemed, for any kind of answer. Which was all the answer he needed.

'Never mind,' he said, and lowered his mouth until her breath, her full wide lips, were soft against his.

Never mind.

CHAPTER SIX

MATTY barely had time to register the fact that she'd been kissed before it was over and Sebastian was on his feet, no doubt already regretting the impulse and anxious to put as much space between them as possible.

'Come on, there's an ice cream van down by the pond,' he said.

Ice cream. Of course. What a pity she hadn't used her brains and kept a safe distance.

Oh, well, it was too late to worry about it. All she could do was ignore her racketing pulse and act as if nothing had happened. 'You really know the way to a woman's heart, Mr Wolseley,' she said, hoping the brightness in her voice didn't sound as forced to him as it did in her own ears.

'You think so?' His voice sounded oddly flat, she thought, but he was staring out across the park so she couldn't see his face. 'Maybe you're right. But in my experience it takes rather more than an ice cream to keep it.'

'I'm sure you've got whatever it takes,' she replied, never doubting that for him it was a well-travelled path.

It took a lot of practice, assurance, to kiss a woman before she knew she wanted to be kissed. To kiss her so that when it was over her lips followed his, wanting more, demanding more.

No one had kissed her that way since the day her car had hit a patch of ice and spun into a wall. And her body, her foolish, traitorous body, had lit up in a response he could not have failed to notice.

Lit up in ways she'd thought were no longer possible. She'd felt…so much. Not just the quick warm flush of sexual desire—her breasts were even now tingling, alive, demanding a lover's touch—but deeper, lower, there had been…something.

Oh, she knew that the brain compensated: touch here, imagine you feel something there. But it had been so much more than that. She wanted it to be more than that. To keep very still. Relive the moment over and over.

But Sebastian had begun to gather the wrappers to dump in a nearby rubbish bin, eager to move on, no doubt wondering what had possessed him. Concerned that a casual kiss might have landed him with a clinging, needy, disabled woman. Certainly wishing he'd stuck to the 'business' part of lunch—or, more likely, that he'd left her to share a sandwich with Blanche.

But, while they'd both probably be more comfortable if she made some excuse and left, the business was too important to allow one momentary—and entirely mutual—lapse of judgement to ruin everything.

She didn't know what Sebastian had been thinking and it didn't matter.

She repeated the words in her head, trying to convince herself at least.

It didn't matter.

If he could pull this off, sell the idea to a major retailer, it would mean that she would have money coming in, regular royalties that she could save towards that home of her own.

That was more important than a little momentary awkwardness. That and securing pensions for Blanche and the rest of the staff.

Those things would continue to matter long after Sebastian Wolseley had returned to New York and forgotten about all of them.

She had to behave as if nothing had happened. Or rather as if being kissed by heart-stoppingly handsome men was such an everyday occurrence for her that she never gave it a second thought.

So she channelled all the feelings, all the magic, into her brightest smile and said, 'Last one to the van buys the ice cream.'

'You want me to race you?' he asked, falling in beside her, close enough to touch, his body a magnet for every cell in her body.

'You think you could win?' Then, 'You know, it seems a shame to waste that sandwich. I'm sure the ducks would appreciate it.'

'What?' Sebastian, still trying to come to terms with a kiss that had left him reeling, forced himself to concentrate. 'Oh, right,' he said, retracing his steps to retrieve it.

He hadn't intended to kiss Matty Lang. There had been none of those carefully choreographed moves that preceded seduction. None of the speaking glances that asked the question, or answered it, ensuring that misunderstandings were avoided.

The sheer spontaneity of that simplest of kisses had served to show him just how controlled his life had been in the last few years.

There had been no artifice, no calculation. It had just seemed…right.

With the memory of the way her lips had clung to his, the scent of her skin overriding the hot, dusty smell of the park, it still seemed that way.

Perfect.

Yet letting go, responding to heart rather than head for

the first time in years, was more than a little frightening.
He would have been hard put to it to say whether his
heart was pounding with desire or terror.

'Are you sure the pickle won't give the ducks indiges-
tion?' he asked, then, when he got no answer, turned to
see Matty speeding away from him along the path.

For one dreadful moment he thought that she'd used
the distraction in order to escape him, but she'd stopped
at the ice cream van and whatever she said to the man
there made him laugh. He belatedly caught up with reality. She'd just pulled a fast one so that she'd get to the
van first.

His kiss might have caught her by surprise—but then
it had taken him much the same way—but she hadn't been
outraged that he'd taken such a blatant liberty. In fact he
was pretty sure that after she'd got over the first momentary shock she'd kissed him back.

In that moment he recognised that, while he wouldn't
deny the terror, for this woman he was prepared to take
the risk and, smiling, went to join her.

She'd already ordered and handed over the money by
the time he joined her. 'Nice move, Matty,' he said. 'But
I thought the loser was going to pay.'

She took her change, leaving him to take the ice cream
cones. 'Unfortunately I lied about the ''loser'' part,' she
said, with a casual lift of her shoulders as she mimicked
his earlier statement about leaving the 'business' out of
lunch. 'Which I guess makes us about even.'

'No. You're a woman. You're always ahead,' he said,
handing her one of the cones before swirling his tongue
around his own ice cream, staring out at the ducks as he
thought about Matty's mouth, cold from the ice cream,
warming beneath his tongue. How that would feel.

Matty let out a tiny sigh of relief. They'd got past the

kiss without toe-curling embarrassment and normal conversation had been resumed. Sebastian, being a man,
would now be able to forget it had ever happened and
they could revert to a working relationship.

She wasn't fooling herself, here.

She didn't believe for a moment that it meant anything
special to him. It was just one of those opportunistic
kisses. Her mouth had been handy and he… Well, she
didn't know what he'd been thinking. Only that all those
powerful *You're a woman… I desire you…* messages his
mouth had appeared to be sending were purely delusional.
Messages she undoubtedly yearned for—just because she
couldn't walk it didn't mean she'd lost any of the desires
or needs natural to an otherwise perfectly healthy woman.

Her brain was simply doing its thing and filling in the
blanks.

All it took was the briefest reality check to remind her
that this was the kind of tester kiss that you might
exchange with a man you fancied. At a party. Or on a
warm sunny afternoon in the park. A kiss that might, or
might not, lead on to something more. Unfortunately there
was no such thing as casual kissing when one of the par-
ticipants couldn't get up and walk away.

But it had been a good kiss, a memorable kiss, and
those were rare enough to be cherished. The trick was
ensuring that Sebastian didn't feel guilty about doing the
walking. Matty didn't want him to think that she might
have taken it as a declaration of…anything.

Nudging her chair nearer to the water, away from him,
declaring her independence, she took the chocolate out of
the ice cream, scooped up a mouthful and bit off the end.

For a moment ice cream and cold chocolate blended,
heated, melted. 'I was thinking about making Toby a

frieze for the playroom,' she said matter-of-factly, be-tween mouthfuls.

It was easy. She'd long since mastered the art of hiding her feelings.

Fairly easy.

'With the alphabet,' she added.

When he didn't answer, she glanced back at him. He seemed more interested in the ducks than in anything she had to say.

'You did ask if I had done anything else for him.'

'So I did. Save it until we get back to the office.'

'I could mock one up for your meeting next week, if you like,' she persisted.

'I'm grateful for all ideas,' he said, finally joining her, settling on the grass beside her, long legs folded up so that his trousers stretched tight against powerful thighs, his elbows propped on his knees. 'But Blanche will get Production to do the mock-ups for you.'

Which, she thought, roughly translated meant he didn't want her involved any more than necessary.

'If that's what you prefer,' she replied, working hard to keep any suggestion that she felt rejected from her voice. Wasn't it what she wanted?

Apparently she'd been kidding herself.

'It's what they're paid for, Matty,' he replied, appar-ently picking up her disappointment.

Hiding her feelings, despite the practice, wasn't so easy after all.

'Oh, don't worry,' she said carelessly, in an effort to recover a little of her self-respect. 'I'll be sure to charge you for every minute of my time.'

'That suits me.' He glanced up at her. 'If I'm paying for your services, I get to choose what you do,' he said, and his voice—soft, practically dripping with innuendo, and rekindling warmth where she shouldn't be feeling anything—warned her not to bait him in this way.

'You do?' she squeaked, then, swallowing hard as she ignored the danger, 'What did you have in mind?'

For a moment their eyes meshed and the risk took shape, coalescing into something hot and dangerous, and if she'd been on her feet she'd have taken a step back.

Or, more likely, thrown herself on him.

Then, as if shutting a door on something private, he momentarily closed his eyes. When he opened them again they were cool, slightly distant, and but for the pounding of the pulse in her throat she could almost have imagined it.

'First,' he said, 'I want you with me when I take a look at the hardware.'

'You do?' Naturally she was interested in seeing it. She might even be able to make some suggestions about layout. But it was clear that too much exposure to Sebastian Wolseley's squeak-inducing presence was not at all wise. She shouldn't even have succumbed to this picnic. The sensible thing would be to keep Blanche between them. And, sensibly, she said, 'I know next to nothing about computer hardware.'

'That's not why I want you with me. It's possible that I'm wrong, but my research leads me to believe that women buy the majority of greetings cards.'

'Then you haven't entirely wasted your time during the last couple of days,' she said, leaving him to decide whether it was the women or their buying habits she thought he was interested in.

'Not entirely,' he admitted. 'Which is why I want to be certain that the hardware is female-friendly.'

'And you need me for that? Surely all you have to do is produce it in pink?' she suggested innocently.

'Excuse me?' He grinned at her. 'Did I just touch a hot button?' He curled his tongue around the ice cream, lighting up buttons that she'd forgotten existed. 'Am I about to get the entire "patronising man" lecture, straight from the feminist handbook?'

She took the precaution of pausing to breathe before attempting to answer him. 'You're familiar with it?'

'Familiar? Like most men of my generation, Matty, I've heard it so many times that I know it by heart.'

'That,' she pointed out, 'is nothing to boast about.'

'It proves I was listening.'

'Clearly not hard enough, or you would only have heard it once.'

'Possibly.' He did the thing with the ice cream again. 'Is this where I have to say that I'm deeply ashamed?'

Matty knew he was deliberately winding her up, but she was so relieved to be feeling an emotion that she didn't have to keep hidden she put all she had into the glare she gave him.

'I wouldn't believe you even if you did,' she replied. 'It is a fact, however, that a very large percentage of women use computers in one guise or another every day, either at work or at home. They aren't likely to be frightened off by something that will probably be simpler to use than the average video recorder.'

'No, ma'am. Point taken.'

'And, since you have been smart enough to recognise that women do account for ninety percent of your sales, I'll let you off the feminist tirade. This time.'

'I'm truly grateful.'

He was definitely winding her up, she decided. In fact she was almost certain that he was enjoying himself. Which was good. They were back on sniping terms. But, deciding that he'd had enough fun at her expense for one day, she said, 'What you really need is a friendly retailer who'll test market the machine for you.'

'That could be tricky. It would have to be an independent trader, and it's possible that if I can interest the big chain buyer I'm seeing next week he'll want an exclusive deal for his stores.'

'All eight hundred of them.'

'As you said, it's a lot of cards.'

'Maybe, but I'm not sure I approve. Independents have a right to make a living, too.'

'I agree. But unfortunately retailing is all about quantity, and the chains can provide that. And the more successful this is, the more money you'll make,' he reminded her.

'You think I'll compromise my ideals out of self-interest?'

'Isn't that the only reason you agreed to have lunch with me? To watch out for your interests.'

She had said something like that; she couldn't deny it. 'It was one of the reasons.' She couldn't remember what the other one was. Apart from a terminally weak will. 'I'll give it some thought, and Fran's brilliant at marketing— maybe she'll come up with some ideas. If you don't mind me discussing your business with her?'

'Not at all. As long as she won't give me grief for interfering with her attempts to find you a publisher.'

'She wouldn't waste the time. She'd just use it as a selling point. After all, if the public buy the cards, they'll buy the book to go with it.'

'Well, okay, then. But I still want you to take a look at the prototype. I know I can rely on you to say what you think. It would never occur to you to consider my feelings if you should spot any flaws in the system.'

'Not for a minute,' she agreed. 'In that case I look forward to it.'

'Are you free on Saturday morning? Or do you have some important commission needing your undivided attention?'

Nothing that wouldn't keep. But in the cause of self-preservation she refused to give him an open-ended invitation to her time, as well as her heart.

'I can spare you a couple of hours first thing. Is that it?'

'No, I want you with me when I meet with the make-or-break buyer. I don't have to tell you how much is riding on its success.'

He didn't. Which was why, much as she regretted doing so, she had to turn this one down.

'You don't want me there, Sebastian.'

'Don't I?'

Sebastian was not particularly surprised at her reluctance. She was outwardly confident, but she'd been doing her best to keep him at arm's length ever since his first call.

It must be so much easier to flirt with a man you're never going to have to see again. To dismiss him with a cutting remark so that you're never left waiting for the phone to ring.

Doing the rejecting to avoid the hurt of being rejected. And he recognised that it would be very easy to hurt her.

He wondered just how many of the people who commissioned her to work for them actually knew she was in a wheelchair.

The phone, the internet, were such useful tools for keeping a safe distance between her and her clients—to protect them from reality, her from prejudice.

But the fact that she couldn't walk did not make her

any less a person. Any less valuable. Quite the contrary. That she'd faced and overcome the problems that everyday life threw at her, with humour and kindness, made her very special.

She needed to know that, too.

'I'm glad you're concerned with what I don't want, Matty.' He finished his ice cream, took his time about sucking the stickiness off his thumb. 'Here I am, sitting in the park on a beautiful day, with a woman I'm having X-rated thoughts about, and the one thing I really don't want to be doing is talking business.'

He turned his head so that he was looking up at her, giving her the chance to put in her five cents' worth, but although her cheeks flushed a warm pink all she could manage was, 'You lied about that.'

'Everyone lies, Matty.'

He waited for her to tell him that he was wrong. That he was just a cynical man who didn't know anything. But she didn't. She wasn't that naïve.

'At least I owned up,' he pointed out. 'You could have left me to eat on my own if you thought you'd been had. Since you chose not to, I hoped you were happy to stay for the company. Unfortunately, you're a tenacious female and just won't quit—'

'What's your point?' she cut in.

'My point is that I'd really rather not spoil the moment by talking about business. But, like the nice guy I am, I'm indulging you—'

'It's *your* business!'

'You don't want to come to lunch next week *because...*' he continued, as if she hadn't interrupted, refusing to let the matter drop and gesturing for her to complete the sentence.

'You're suggesting I should "indulge" you in return, Mr Nice Guy?'

'It seems only fair.'

'Oh…' She waved what was left of her own ice cream cone in the direction of the pond, presumably hoping to distract him from the hot blush that was searing her cheeks. 'Go feed the ducks.'

'Better,' he said, grinning as he tore a piece off the sandwich and tossed it into the water, causing a minor commotion as the birds dived on it. 'Much better.' Then, because he couldn't resist it, he said, 'Do you know, I do believe you've caught the sun?'

'Is Matty not with you?' Blanche asked, following him into his office.

Sebastian picked up the pile of messages left on his desk and began to sort through them. The journalists had not given up, he noticed. That was good. He would use them in his own good time. Some free publicity in return for all the column inches he'd given them in the past would even the score a little.

'No. I've worked out how we can use her illustrations.' He briefly explained what he had in mind. 'It means some changes to the artwork and, since there isn't much time, she's gone straight home to get on with it.'

He'd anticipated Blanche would respond with doom-laden objections to his idea, but instead she just said, 'Matty's a lovely woman.'

'I think so.'

'But vulnerable.'

He considered the ease with which she appeared to get around in her chair, unfazed by traffic or crowds of pedestrians, all of whom towered over her. The competence with which she managed her specially adapted car.

He knew it couldn't be that simple, but then that wasn't what Blanche had meant by vulnerable.

'And your point is?'

For a moment he thought she was going to back down, let it go. But her protective instincts had always been stronger than those of self-preservation and she said, 'I saw the way she looked at you, Sebastian. I know you can't help how she feels, but you shouldn't encourage her. It isn't fair.'

'She isn't you, Blanche,' he said, smothering the flash of anger that she could think him so shallow. It had taken guts to say what she had. And it was Matty she was stepping up to protect. 'And I'm not George.'

'Maybe not.' She blushed a little, but stood her ground. 'But it would be kinder to cut out picnics in the park and stick strictly to business.'

Pretty much what Matty had said herself.

'I hope you've got a little spare empathy for me, Blanche.' Then, when she didn't leap to assure him, 'If you'd been looking in the other direction, you would have seen how I was looking at her, and believe me, whatever she's feeling, Matty is doing a very good job of keeping me at a safe distance.'

Blanche just looked at him for a moment, then said, 'Don't hurt her, Sebastian.'

She didn't expect him to answer her, didn't wait for him to answer her. But when she'd left him to ponder what she'd said it occurred to Sebastian that he needed to know a lot more about what Matty's life entailed.

Sisters were, as she herself had implied, occasionally useful. And he dialled the number of the London teaching hospital where he hoped to find the oldest and the brainiest of his siblings at her desk.

CHAPTER SEVEN

MATTY hadn't slept particularly well. She'd worked late into the evening on the computer, adapting her illustrations so that there was room for a child's name, and adding in tiny details that would frame the cards to give them a more finished look.

The concentration was supposed to act in the same way as a draught excluder, but, instead of preventing cold draughts, its purpose was to prevent Sebastian Wolseley from seeping under her guard and getting into her thoughts.

Except, of course, like a draught, he was impossible to keep out.

She'd been fine until she'd reached the letter X, but then he'd been there, with his X-rated thoughts and the vivid memory of a kiss that had provoked unexpected, unwanted, X-rated thoughts of her own.

Not that he'd brought up the subject again. He hadn't said or done anything to suggest either was at the forefront of his mind as they'd fed the ducks, then wandered slowly back through the park towards the office.

Instead he'd turned the conversation to music, art, searching out interests, tastes they might have in common. They'd argued amiably over their differences—he thought Tchaikovsky was too romantic; she thought Wagner was too loud—but they both liked Mozart and modern jazz and Frank Sinatra, which successfully cancelled out all other musical disagreements.

And, while she thought he was a little unkind about the

Pre-Raphaelites, their tastes in modern art pleasingly co-incided.

She'd asked him about New York, why he'd made the move. Stupid question. Given the chance she'd have loved to spend time there. She'd expected him to tell her that he'd been head-hunted by the bank, but by that time they'd reached her car and, instead of indulging her curiosity, he'd asked, 'Is there anything I can do to help?'

'No, thanks. I can manage,' she said, trying not to feel self-conscious, or make a mess of operating the lift that slotted her and her chair behind the wheel of her specially adapted car. It was something she normally did on automatic, without having to think about what she was doing. With Sebastian watching she felt all fingers and thumbs.

Awkward.

Disabled.

It brought home the fact that, no matter how much they had in common, all it took was this one single difference between them to make all the X-rated thoughts in the world superfluous.

Which was a jolly good thing, she decided as, gripping the steering wheel, she turned to say goodbye. The more he understood the reality of her life, the less inclined he'd be towards X-rated anything.

And that simple demonstration of reality appeared to work.

She anticipated a brotherly kiss on the cheek as he said goodbye—the kind he'd given Fran. Steeled herself not to mind the difference between that and the mind-blowing heat of the kiss he'd stolen in the park.

But he didn't even do that. He just lightly covered her hand with his own for a moment.

It was enough. Whatever power emanated from him—firing up her body, jump-starting feelings that were better left undisturbed—worked just as well hand-to-hand as it did mouth-to-mouth.

One touch, the barest hint of a smile.

'Will you bring the disk with the changes?'

'I've got too much to do. I'll send it with a courier.'

She thought he'd give her an argument, but he didn't. Just said, 'Give Blanche a call. She'll organise it.'

She swallowed, telling herself it was foolish to be disappointed. This was what she wanted.

'I'll do that.'

'Until Saturday, then. Is eight too early for you?'

She shook her head. 'Eight is fine.'

With one last touch to her hand, he turned and walked away. Using her wing mirror, she watched him until he was out of sight. Then she started the car and, quite deliberately blocking him from her thoughts, gave her full attention to the road.

She was good at blocking out the stuff she didn't want to think about. Didn't want to remember.

There was plenty to block.

But that X took her by surprise. She was quite happily fixing the W and then, when it was done and she moved on to the next letter, there he was. And, instead of X is for Xebec, her head was filled with that image of Sebastian Wolseley, his tongue swirling around the ice cream.

X-rated.

She did her best to ignore him, working one step at a time, adjusting the layout, adding the frame, moving on to the final two letters before copying the whole thing onto a disk for him.

It was late, the day had been hectic, but even when she finally got her pillows placed so that she could sleep comfortably, her dreams wouldn't leave her in peace. Instead, they were filled with all the Xs she'd found in the dictionary as she'd hunted for something a little boy would like.

She'd discarded xylophone as being too obvious, X-rays as being a little scary, and Xmas as being just plain tacky, finally settling on a small three-masted Mediterranean ship called a xebec.

They were all there, but in her dreams the ship's captain was Sebastian Wolseley; he was flying a skull and cross-bones and she knew he was coming to steal her heart...

Now, she put herself through her exercise programme with more than usual vigour, using the standing table to keep her lower body as used to weight bearing as it could ever be, hand-pedalling the recumbent bike to move her legs, working her arms and shoulders until they burned.

The physio had encouraged her to try more, but she'd used the excuse that she scarcely had enough room for the equipment she already had.

Everyone lies.

But she was safe enough. He wasn't coming to steal her heart. There was no need. He already had it in the palm of his hand.

Fine. He could keep it. She had no use for it, after all. And she picked up the phone and called Blanche to tell her that the disk was ready to be picked up.

She was gathering the paperwork to attack her tax return when the doorbell rang.

She picked up the entry phone and said, 'Yes?' She assumed it was the courier, but was taking no chances.

'Courier. Pick up for Coronet?'

She'd half expected Sebastian to come himself, but the voice was reassuringly Scottish and she buzzed him in, before crossing to her workstation to fetch the package containing the disk.

'You know, you really should have a video link on that door,' Sebastian said, still using the Scottish accent. But in the same room he'd never fool her. 'I could have been anyone.'

'You *are* anyone,' she declared, furious at being duped. Furious that he'd known he'd need to dupe her to get in. She spun around, determined to give him a piece of her mind, but was momentarily distracted by the fact that he was wearing the kind of worn soft, close-fitting jeans that there should be a law against. Then, with commendable strength of will, she redirected her gaze from his hips to his face and said, 'Haven't you got anything better to do with your time than run errands?'

'I'm taking the disk straight down to my brother-in-law. He's got the software engineer standing by. Is that it?' he asked.

'Yes,' she managed, regretting her outburst and feeling extremely stupid as she handed him the package. 'Sorry.'

'Don't be. I love it when you blush.' Then, 'Why don't you come with me?'

'Where?'

'Josh is using his private workshop for this. It's quite near the coast. We could go on once we've dropped this off. Have some—'

'No!' she snapped, before he could say the word. While she was still mad enough at his deception to refuse. Already the fact that he'd made the effort was beginning to feel more like flattery... 'Thank you, but I've got a very heavy schedule for the rest of the week.'

'Really? Blanche said you were working on your accounts.'

'In my book, that's heavy.'

'I'd do it for you in return for dinner.'

'I can't cook,' she lied.

'Who said anything about you doing the cooking? But I won't press you. I can see that you'd much rather spend the day sorting out your invoices than strolling along the prom with—'

'I don't "stroll",' she pointed out.

He shrugged. 'Just a figure of speech. I stroll; you roll.'

'So I do. It sounds almost too good to miss, but I'll contain my disappointment somehow.'

That just provoked a grin. 'Only until Saturday.'

'Make sure you shut the door on your way out.'

An hour later Fran brought down an engineer to upgrade Matty's entryphone to one with a video link. 'Guy felt you'd be safer if you could see who was at the door before you opened it,' she explained.

Matty just about managed not to laugh.

'Guy said that? When?'

'He rang from his office. Apparently he was talking to someone about a friend who'd been tricked into opening the door by a phoney delivery man.'

'How dreadful. What did he want?'

'Who?'

'The phoney delivery man.'

'Oh. I don't know. Guy didn't say.'

What a surprise...

'Actually, whatever it was must have been pretty bad because we're having one fitted, too.'

Fran sounded utterly sincere, and quite obviously believed that this was all her adorable husband's idea—which, of course, made it impossible to say that she didn't want it.

Clever Sebastian.

But not that clever. Once it was installed, she wouldn't be tricked into opening the door to any more phoney couriers. Whether they were Sebastian or not.

'Do tell Guy I said thank you, won't you? I really appreciate his concern, but I insist on paying my share.'

'Oh, right. That's going to happen.'

'Maybe I should ask the engineer to have the company bill me separately?'

'Fighting talk. I dare you to come to supper tonight and tell Guy that to his face.'

'Supper?' The bottled-up laughter exploded.

'What's so funny?'

'Tell me, Fran, do I look as if I need a square meal?'

'No.' Then, clearly bemused at this response to her invitation, 'What makes you ask that?'

Matty shook her head. 'No reason. It's just that everyone I've met lately wants to feed me.'

'Lucky you. Anyone special?' Fran prompted, putting a stop to Matty's giggles.

'No,' she said. 'No one special. Just work.'

'Oh, well, that's a shame. But it beats cooking. My advice, for what it's worth, is to go for it.'

'I'll bear that in mind.'

'And in the meantime come up to us tonight. Not that I'm planning anything more exciting than pasta, but we'll eat out on the verandah while this weather holds, and I'll open a bottle of something cheerful. I've hardly seen you since the reception.'

'We've both been busy.'

And life upstairs had changed out of all recognition now that Guy was home and baby Stephanie had arrived. So much to remind her of all she could never have.

A pretty feeble excuse by any standard.

She needed to get over it. Start counting her blessings. She had friends, family who cared about her, and a God-given talent that meant she was able to earn a living from her own home.

And Sebastian? What about him?

'Come up about seven,' Fran said, breaking into her thoughts. 'You can tell me about all these people who want to feed you.'

After Fran had gone, Matty wondered whether Sebastian would turn up there, too. Then she told herself not to be paranoid.

It didn't stop her applying her make-up with more than usual care. Or viewing the result with considerably less than satisfaction. She had another go at her hair. She'd grown it longer for the wedding, wanting to look more feminine, more like a real bridesmaid. Styled by a hairdresser who knew what she was doing, it had worked. For a day.

She tugged a comb through an errant curl that seemed to have a will of its own. It irritated the life out of her and she was constantly wrapping it around her finger to keep it out of the way when she was thinking. Or as a distraction when she was trying not to.

It was retaliating now by refusing to lie down.

She desperately applied hair gel in an attempt to tame it. Five minutes later it was still sticking up, only now stiff with the gel. She looked like a startled hen.

'Cluck,' she said, laughing at herself. What on earth did she think she was doing? Tarting herself up on the off-chance that Sebastian would turn up for supper?

Did she think for one moment that if she was wearing lipstick, if her hair looked tidy for once, he might forget that she couldn't walk?

She reached for the nail scissors lying on her dressing table, still laughing, even though tears seemed to be pouring down her cheeks, and with a low, 'Cluck, cluck, cluck,' she caught hold of the curl and sliced through it.

Curl after curl followed it, until the floor around her

chair was dark with her hair. The laughter had long since died, and the sound of the doorbell cut into a silence so deep that even the traffic in the street outside seemed to have stopped.

The sound brought everything sharply back into focus. She saw the scissors in her hand, and then herself in the mirror. Face white, mouth a vivid red. Her hair…

She closed her eyes to block out the sight of herself, to squeeze back the tears. There was no point in crying. There was nothing left to weep for.

She dropped the scissors, crossed to the new phone with its tiny screen, turned it on and there was Sebastian, looking into the camera as if he knew she was there, watching him…

'Go away,' she begged beneath her breath, rubbing the wetness from her cheeks with the palm of her hand. 'Please, just go away…' And she turned off the video link, unable to bear the pain of looking at him.

She half expected the bell to ring again, was holding her breath when, after the longest pause, she heard the sound of something being pushed through the letterbox.

That was it?

He'd given up that easily?

It was unreasonable to feel angry. After all, she had the camera now. If she was there, she knew who was at the door. And if she didn't open it, it was because she didn't want to.

He hadn't given up. He'd accepted her decision.

He'd listened.

Which was good. But when she went to the door she touched it, as if the connection would still be there…

Stupid. She'd done the right thing.

He didn't want her. He mustn't want her. There were

men—gentle, quiet men—who might be able to live with the limitations of her life, but, like Sebastian, she needed more than that. That was why she knew that he needed someone who would be a complete match for him, physically as well as mentally.

He was just confusing pity with something deeper, and she didn't want to be responsible for how he'd feel when he finally realised that. Didn't want to witness him attempting to extricate himself from their relationship without hurting her or hating himself.

She'd seen one good man do that, and she refused to put another through the same nightmare.

There was absolutely no need to see him again.

She'd done everything she could for Coronet. From now on she'd be out to casual callers and she'd leave the answering machine on so that she couldn't be ambushed by his voice. And she'd be too busy to get involved in any more 'consultancy' work, too. If he needed her to do any more work on the illustrations he'd have to deal with her by e-mail.

She lifted the flap on the basket that caught her mail and took out the large brown envelope he'd pushed through the door. There was nothing on the envelope, it wasn't even sealed, and, opening it to look inside, she saw that it contained greetings cards.

She tipped them out onto her lap.

Her cards.

She picked each one up and looked at it. 'J is for Josh'. 'B is for Beatrice'. 'D is for Danny'.

'S is for Sebastian'.

Josh was his brother-in-law. But who was Beatrice? And Danny?

There was a brief note on the back of the 'S is for...' card.

Matty, I would have 'made me a willow cabin at your gate', but I've got something else planned for tonight that I can't cancel. In the meantime, here are the results so far.
Sebastian.

Something else? Doing what? If he'd been going to supper with Fran and Guy he would have come down through the garden to bring her the cards himself. He wasn't a man who understood the meaning of the word no.

None of your business, Matty, she told herself, trying not to feel jealous, to wonder if he'd already been distracted by some girl he could look in the eye without getting on his knees. Took a reality check.

Then looked again at the note, tracing the bold handwriting with a fingertip... A willow cabin?

She vaguely recognised it as a quote from something. Something from school. Fran would know what it was; she'd always been better at that kind of stuff.

Catching sight of herself in the hall mirror, she gave a little gasp. There was no way she could go upstairs looking like this. She'd have to phone her anyway to cry off supper—say that she'd got a last-minute commission with a tight deadline. If she told her she was tired she'd just come rushing down to fuss over her, and she didn't want anyone seeing her with her hair like this, especially not Fran. She'd take one look and know...

'A willow cabin?' Fran repeated, a few minutes later. 'It's Shakespeare. *Twelfth Night*... Don't you remember? Olivia asks Viola what she'd do if she loved someone who wouldn't listen to her, and... Hold on...' There was muffled sound as a hand was placed over the receiver, then she said, 'I'll look it up and you can see for yourself when you come up.'

'No, that's why I rang. I've just had a fax about that illustration I did earlier in the week. They want some changes and it has to be with them first thing in the morning.'

'Oh, right. Well, if you've got to work we'll do it another night.'

'Of course.' Then, 'The quotation?'

'Oh, right. As far as I can remember it goes something like, "Make me a willow cabin—"'

'"Make me a willow cabin at your gate, And call upon my soul within the house; Write loyal cantons of contemnèd love, And sing them loud..."'

She dropped the phone and swung round to face Sebastian, who was standing in the French windows, looking like some kind of a god in a dinner jacket...

'Stop it!' she cried.

'"...even in the dead of night."'

'Don't!' Then, 'Please, Sebastian, don't do this. I can't bear it,' she said, betraying all the feelings she'd been at such pains to hide.

He didn't ask her what she wanted him to stop doing, but crossed the room, picked up the phone, and said, 'It's okay, Fran,' before replacing it on the cradle.

'It isn't okay!'

It was anything but okay. But his only response was to lightly run his hand over her hair and say, 'Do you want to tell me what happened?'

'Nothing. I'm just having a bad hair day, that's all.'

He didn't take his hand away, but left it resting lightly on her nape. It felt so perfect there. So reassuring...

'A bad hair day?'

'That curl just wouldn't lie down.'

'So you killed it?'

'That's right.' Making him laugh was the answer. If she could make him laugh he might just forget that desperate cry. 'Now you know the awful truth. I'm a curl-murderer…'

He smiled, but it wasn't the ha-ha-ha kind of smile she'd been aiming for. It was heartbreakingly tender, full of concern, and although his hand slid from her neck it was only to take both her hands in his as he knelt in front of her.

'I didn't mean today, Matty. You've done that before, haven't you?'

What on earth had Fran been telling him? How dared she?

'In Fran's office, upstairs, there's a photograph of the two of you—taken when you were students, I imagine.'

She knew the picture. Fran had a board with dozens of photographs pinned to it. Most were newer—of the children, Guy, his brother Steven—but there were one of the two of them taken when they'd gone backpacking around Europe after graduation, in those last few months before life was meant to begin in earnest. Two laughing girls with their whole lives ahead of them.

'What were you doing in Fran's office?' she demanded.

'The key to Guy's apartment was in the safe. We sat there for a while talking, having a drink, trying to work out what had happened to the last ten years. You had long hair then. Down to your waist.'

'Since when has it been a crime to cut your hair?' She knew as soon as the words had left her mouth that she'd overreacted. She would have made one of those careless, dismissive gestures if he hadn't been holding on to her hands, but she tried for the effect with, 'It's no big deal,

Sebastian. I just couldn't manage it after the accident, that's all.'

'So you sat in front of a mirror and hacked it off?'

Was he guessing? Or had Fran told Guy the whole sorry story?

'Is that what happened?' he asked.

There was a lump in her throat, and despite the fact that she wanted to tell him to leave her alone, stop bothering her, stop forcing herself to think about what had happened, her tongue refused to work.

'Trust me, Matty,' he said.

Trust him? To do what? Listen to what she'd done and still look at her as if he cared?

And then, realising that was the answer—to tell him everything—she said, 'I was pregnant.'

The words were muffled by her thick tongue, the lump in her throat. She swallowed it down and said it again. 'When I skidded into that brick wall I was pregnant. I didn't just lose the use of my legs. I killed my baby.'

CHAPTER EIGHT

SEBASTIAN let go of her hands, stood up, walked away.

She closed her eyes so that she wouldn't have to watch him leave. It was what she wanted, what she'd made happen, but she felt as if she'd been cast adrift on a cold, dark sea.

'Here.'

Startled, she looked up. 'I thought you'd gone.'

'Think again.' He took her hand, wrapped it around a glass, holding them there with his own hands. 'Drink this.'

She looked down and realised she was holding a glass of brandy.

'I don't—'

'You do now,' he said again, gently but firmly. No argument accepted. 'I'm prescribing this on purely medicinal grounds.'

'You're not a doctor.'

'No, but I'm asking you to trust me anyway.'

Trust me…

Could she do that?

Not even wanting to contemplate the idea, she took a mouthful of the brandy, spluttering as the spirit caught the back of her throat.

'Gently,' he cautioned. 'A sip at a time.'

Then, when he was sure that she had the glass safely, he took a mobile phone from his pocket and made a call. 'James? Sebastian Wolseley. Will you please pass my regrets to the chairman? Tell him I won't be able to make the dinner this evening—'

'No,' she gasped, her vocal cords apparently anaesthetised by the brandy.

'A family emergency,' he continued, taking no notice. 'Thank you.'

'No,' she repeated, more forcefully. He wasn't supposed to stay. 'What have you done?'

'Bailed out of a tedious dinner with a group of boring businessmen,' he said.

'You weren't having supper with Fran and Guy?'

'A little overdressed for that, wouldn't you say?' Then, as he tugged on his black tie, unfastened the stud, he said, 'Okay now?'

'You shouldn't be here.'

'You think I'm leaving with only half the story?' He took the glass from her, then leaned forward and put his hands to her waist.

'What are you doing?'

'Moving you to the sofa so that I can put my arm around you while you finish what you started.'

This wasn't supposed to happen.

It was clear that she had only two choices. Let him lift her, hold her. Or do it herself.

'I'm not useless,' she said, waving him away. 'I can manage. You can keep your arm to yourself.'

For a moment he stayed exactly where he was, then, as if he realised she was serious, he stepped back, and she crossed to the sofa, leaned forward to grab the back of it and pulled herself up, turning as she fell against the cushions. It wasn't graceful, but it worked.

'Have you eaten?' he asked, moving her chair to the side of the sofa, where she could reach it if she needed it.

'What? No. Don't mollycoddle me, Sebastian. I'm not worth it.' Then, realising that he had just sacrificed his own banquet, she said, 'If you're hungry I'm sure the boring businessmen will be glad to learn that your "family emergency" was not as serious as first thought.'

He ignored the jibe, removed his jacket, and then, without so much as a by-your-leave, he picked her up, so that he could claim the space next to the arm, and settled her beside him with her feet up, her body pressed against him, his arm very definitely around her.

'I'm sorry that you lost your baby, Matty.'

'I hate it when people say that. "Lost your baby." It sounds as if you've put it down somewhere and can't remember when you left it. I didn't mislay my baby, Sebastian. I killed it.'

'You had an accident. Skidded on a patch of ice.'

She'd told him that. That 'speed, black ice, brick wall' line was her way of dismissing the subject. 'It was my fault. I wasn't paying attention—'

'You've paid a high price, Matty. I think you might give yourself a break on the guilt.'

'Really?' She half turned to look up at him. 'You think so?' He met her challenge with a look of such compassion that she very nearly broke down and wept. But self-pity was so very unattractive. And so little deserved. 'I think I know best what kind of break I deserve.'

Turning away, because that look was really getting to her, she said, 'Isn't this where you ask me about the father?'

'I don't know. This isn't the kind of stuff I normally do.' Then, 'Where the hell is he, anyway?'

'Happily married to a very nice woman. They're expecting a baby any day.'

'He thought you'd want to know that?'

'His mother wrote to me at Christmas. She didn't want me to hear it from just anyone. She simply wanted...'

She'd wanted to thank her, but Matty couldn't say that. If she told him that he'd know. But she heard, felt, Sebastian's sharp intake of breath as his quick brain made the leap and worked it out for himself.

'Tell me, was it very difficult to get him to walk away?' he asked, and she began to shiver, despite the warmth of his body, his arm around her. It wasn't from cold though; it was fear.

It was frightening just how well this man understood her. He made her feel like glass: transparent, fragile.

'Will you shut the door on your way out, Sebastian?' she said, making a determined effort to put space between them.

'How difficult?' he persisted, tightening his hold, refusing to let her go.

'Not nearly as difficult as it is to get rid of you,' she declared, and, because nothing else would move him, 'Listen to me, Sebastian. I killed my baby. The accident was my fault. I was criminally negligent.'

'Were you speeding?'

'What?' Wasn't that enough for him? 'No, I wasn't speeding—'

'Over the legal alcohol limit?'

'It was eight o'clock in the morning! I was on my way to work...' She gave a shuddering sigh. 'I was using my mobile phone, Sebastian. Trying to call Michael to tell him the news. I just couldn't wait to tell him that he was going to be a father.'

He said nothing, but there was warmth by her ear as he brushed his lips against her temple. A comfort kiss. That was all...

'I was so stupid. It hadn't even occurred to me that I might be pregnant. I'd had no morning sickness, no symptoms, and I'd put the missed period down to the upset at

Michael going away. His company had sent him to Chile to work on a bridge project,' she explained.

'We'd had a brief holiday before he went away. A week at a cottage beside the sea. Nothing exciting. Just walks on the beach—it was late autumn, too cold to swim, but the weather was bright, the hillsides purple with heather.'

They'd walked, talked about the future, made love.

Made their baby.

The words tumbled out of her. How they'd met at a party and how the world had suddenly all seemed to fall into place, as if she'd found a missing jigsaw puzzle piece and finally could see the whole picture.

'That's how it is when you meet the right person,' Sebastian said. 'It's as if you've spent your whole life trying to ram a round peg into a square hole. And then, suddenly, it all fits.'

She turned to look up at him. He knew. Of course he did. No man reached his mid-thirties without losing his heart at least once.

'Yes, that's how it is,' she said. How it was. When you loved someone you didn't hang on to him when you were drowning, pull him under with you just because you were scared witless.

'I'd been feeling just a bit tired, that was all, and I decided to go to work early so that I could stop at the pharmacy in the twenty-four-hour supermarket, pick up some vitamins.' The memory was so vivid. It was as if she was there. Staring at the shelf. 'I was waiting to pay for them when I found myself staring at a pregnancy testing kit. It was as if I'd been sleepwalking and I was suddenly awake. I bought the kit, rushed to a loo and there it was. Our baby.'

His arm tightened imperceptibly, as if he knew how

much it was hurting to remember, to tell him, and he was trying to hold her together. Lend her his strength.

'I was so excited. So thrilled. I just wanted Michael to be there so that I could share what I was feeling. I did the next best thing. I sat in the car park and called him.

'It would have been the early hours in Chile, surely?'

'I thought he might wake up. But his phone was turned off, and it isn't the kind of message you can leave on a voicemail. You have to be together, even if "together" is courtesy of some communications satellite.'

She closed her eyes, remembering the elation, the joy. 'It was such a beautiful day, Sebastian. Freezing cold, but crystal-clear. The sky was that pinky blue you get just before the sun actually appears above the horizon. I could see my breath condensing in the cold, and everything was sparkling with frost, and I thought... This is magic. I was so happy and I thought, I'll call again. Leave a message so that the first voice he hears in the morning is mine. Ask him to call me the minute he's awake...' And somehow Sebastian had both arms around her and her tears were soaking his shirt. 'The phone was there, on the seat beside me, the road was clear and I only looked away for a second...'

And then the sound of her tyres on the road had changed from a rumble to a hiss, the steering had gone slack and she had been heading straight for a brick wall.

'When I regained consciousness my baby was gone and Michael was sitting by my bed. I didn't know what had happened, but he was crying, and I sort of knew that his tears weren't just for me, or our baby, but for himself.'

'My heart bleeds for him,' Sebastian said. He sounded angry, but that wasn't right...

'No. I understood. And he was really supportive, really upbeat about the future. He wanted to give up the job in

Chile, come home so that he could stay with me, help me through rehab.'

'But?'

'But it was a fabulous job, and what could he do? Really? It was going to be months, and there was absolutely no point in him giving up everything to sit and twiddle his thumbs.'

'So you sent him back to work.'

'He couldn't do anything for me.'

'He could have been there.'

She swallowed. 'If the baby had survived—well, maybe things would have been different.' Maybe. He'd said all the right things, but she'd seen the fear in his eyes as he'd looked into a future he hadn't bargained for. Didn't want.

'And?'

'After a couple of months I wrote and told him I'd met someone else. A therapist at the rehab centre.'

'He believed you? Just accepted it? Didn't he know you at all?'

'He must have had his doubts because he asked his mother to come and see me. She took one look and she certainly knew that I was lying. She hugged me and cried and said…' Matty discovered she could think about it now without breaking down. 'She said, "Thank you."'

'Oh, God.'

'No, no… Don't you see? Michael fell in love with this girl he'd met who magically loved to do all the things he enjoyed. Rock-climbing. Sailing. Walking. He didn't change; I did. If it had happened after we'd married he'd have coped, lived with it. He was a good man, but I didn't want him making that kind of sacrifice for me, Sebastian.'

'You think his life with you would have been second class in some way?'

'He's got a wife, a baby coming. A whole life—'

'Is there any reason why you can't have children? Didn't one of those Olympic wheelchair athletes have a baby and then come back and win gold again?'

'Yes, but it isn't an issue, Sebastian. I had my chance and threw it away in a moment of carelessness.'

'If we were only allowed one chance to get it right, Matty, the human race wouldn't get very far.'

Painful as the subject was, at least he seemed to have forgotten all about her hair—the reason she'd attacked it with the nail scissors. At least she hoped he'd forgotten. Because it wouldn't take him long to work out that hacking it off in the bathroom that day in the rehab centre had been a symbolic gesture. Severing herself from all that was womanly, alluring in her appearance. A denial of her very femininity.

And then he'd know why she'd done it again today.

So much for keeping him away.

She rubbed her palm over her cheek and with a determined attempt at a smile said, 'You're right. In your case, you'd starve to death. I'll go and clean up and then I'll sort out some food.'

Sebastian didn't want to move, but to stay just where he was with his arms wrapped around Matty. It had taken him long enough to get her there, and they'd moved so far forward in one night. The rest would keep. He kissed the top of her poor, abused hair.

Actually, he didn't need her to explain about that. It was easy enough to work out that when she was angry, frightened, pushing away the people who loved her, she chopped off her hair.

That she'd done it today didn't make him feel rejected, it just made him feel stronger, more confident of winning her—because she wouldn't have done it unless she cared.

She'd tried to push him away, but he was still here. And she was offering him food.

A bit of a switch there.

'I have to admit it's been a while since lunch,' he said. 'But don't bother unless you're going to join me.'

There was the briefest pause before she said, 'Of course I'm going to have something.' Then, 'Sit back, make yourself at home, and be prepared to be amazed as I conjure up one of the culinary masterpieces of the world.'

'I thought you said you couldn't cook,' he said, just about managing to stop himself protesting as she leaned forward, out of the safety of his arms. She didn't need him to keep her safe. She was capable, strong. Maybe he'd be more usefully occupied in demonstrating to her just how strong. And he thought about the picture she'd been working on. The fact that she'd rejected Fran's offer of a trip to the sea...

'Who said anything about cooking?' she replied, reaching for the phone and scrolling through numbers. 'Take your pick. Indian? Chinese? Italian?'

He took the phone from her. 'What have you got in your fridge?'

'The usual stuff. What's your point?'

'My point, my darling, is that any fool can summon up a pizza with a phone and a credit card, but I have this desperate urge to demonstrate that not all men are a useless waste of space—'

'Are you calling me a fool?'

'—and, if you're very lucky, I'll let you do the chopping and slicing.'

'Where exactly are we going?' Matty asked briskly, when he arrived early on Saturday morning.

She hadn't seen or spoken to him since the night she'd tried to drive him away.

That had been a success. Not.

Instead he'd cooked her the most amazing spaghetti carbonara, before kissing her goodnight on her forehead as if she were about six years old.

It seemed, from the lack of any further invitations to lunch, dinner or other engagement involving food, that he'd regretted encouraging her to purge her emotions all over his dress shirt.

She didn't blame him one bit. If he'd listened to her... But he hadn't.

Whatever. The only reason he was here now was because he needed her to put the finishing touches to the cards. Purely business. Just what she'd wanted.

She could be as brisk, distant, businesslike as the next woman. Just to prove it, she said, 'I'll follow you. But I'd better have the address just in case I lose you—'

'Follow me?' he interrupted.

Oh, yes. She didn't need pirates invading her dreams to get the message that sharing an enclosed space with him for any length of time would be plain stupid. She'd lain against his chest with his heart beating beneath her cheek. She understood the danger.

The only reason she was doing this was because of Blanche and the rest of the Coronet staff. And maybe just a little bit for herself. She had her own future to think of. Which did not—*did not*—include Sebastian Wolseley.

'Why would you want to follow me?' he asked, clearly bemused by the suggestion.

'I'm just thinking of you,' she said. 'Of course you're welcome to travel with me, if you like, but I know most men loath being driven by a woman, and I don't have that good a record—'

'I appreciate your thoughtfulness, but frankly I feel pretty uneasy being driven by some men. It's not the sex of the driver I object to, it's the way they drive. Somehow I doubt that you'll be letting your attention wander.'

'Especially if that woman is using hand controls,' she finished, once he'd got that off his chest. 'I promise you I won't be offended if you'd rather not.'

'Hands, feet—I'm sure you know what you're doing. But what's the problem with me driving you?'

'Didn't you notice the way my car is set up the other day?'

'It's adapted for your wheelchair. So?'

'Exactly. No driver's seat. I'm the only person who can drive it.'

'I realise that. I didn't mean I should drive your car. On the contrary, I assumed you would come in mine.'

Of course he did. He was a man. Arrogance came as a standard accessory.

'Unfortunately it isn't that simple,' she said, wishing she didn't always have to explain this. 'For a start, some cars are easier to get into and out of than others.'

With the lift system on her own car she didn't have to worry about that.

And then, of course, there was that other thing. That thing about surrendering all control over the way she moved to someone else. As his passenger, she'd be utterly reliant on Sebastian. He'd have to cope with her wheelchair, help her manoeuvre in and out of a car she wasn't familiar with.

She might even have to hold on to him while he lifted her from the car to her chair.

He had no idea.

And she was done with up-close-and-personal.

'That might be a problem,' she said. 'My wheelchair

takes up rather a lot of room. You did say the car you'd
borrowed was old?'

'I did. I didn't say it was a small.'

'No, but—'

'If I can get your chair in without difficulty, will you
come with me?'

Short of coming right out and telling him straight that
she didn't want to ride with him, there didn't seem to be
any way of avoiding it.

'All right,' she said. 'It's a deal.'

All she had to lose was her dignity—and she'd lost that,
along with the use of her legs, long enough ago to be used
to it.

Sebastian, on the other hand, would certainly learn a
thing or two about her life. Actually, maybe it wasn't such
a bad idea after all...

'I'll meet you out front,' she said.

'You will?'

'The steps,' she reminded him. 'I have to go out the
back way.' It wasn't unusual. In her time she'd been in
goods lifts, through trade entrances—all around the pro-
verbial houses rather than through the front door—just to
get to where she needed to go.

'Well, hold on. Hadn't I better try the wheelchair first?'

Good idea. A better one would be for her to stop making excuses to do what he wanted.

Get a grip, Matty...

'You know, it would really be a lot easier if we just
reverted to my first idea. You said you were going to be
down there all day, and I really need to get back. I never
did get my paperwork done—'

'All work and no play is very bad for you.'

'Paperwork is important,' she declared. 'Besides, this
is work.'

He smiled. 'Of course it is. And much more important than filing your receipts, so let's make a move.'

And, with that, he leaned down, slid his hands under her arms, then, when, startled, she just sat there looking up at him, he said, 'This would be much so easier if you would put your arms around my neck.'

'What…? I don't need you—'

'Trust me, Matty,' he said. But, perhaps deciding that was one appeal too far, he didn't hang around for an argument. 'I know what I'm doing.' And he lifted her clear off the chair.

Her arms—not taking one bit of notice of her 'whats' and 'don'ts'—took the sensible course and flung themselves around his neck, and before she knew it she was vertical, upright, Sebastian's arms holding her safe against his chest. And for a heartbeat she was any girl in any man's arms.

Then reality intruded. 'This isn't…' she began. 'You can't… I shouldn't…'

The words to tell him what it was exactly that he couldn't, she shouldn't do, failed her, and, very softly, he said, 'We can do anything we want, Matty.' Then, 'It's not so bad, is it?'

Bad?

His breath was warm on her cheek, his face just inches from her own.

Oh, this was bad. About as bad as it could be.

His hand at her waist was pressing her close to him, so that there was nothing but thin silk and soft cotton between her skin and his. Her imagination instantly filled the gap, her breasts engorging, her nipples tightening as feminine instincts as old as time urged her to go for broke and kiss him, caress him, draw him to her and never let him go.

So much for all her good intentions.

Could he feel her response to him?

Did he know what effect he had on her?

A smile that began somewhere behind his eyes and slowly filled his entire face was all the answer she needed.

'Wanna dance, lady?' he murmured.

She closed her eyes. He was a man who understood his power, used it ruthlessly. Of course he knew.

She couldn't look at him, couldn't answer him, and instead, biting down on her lip to stop herself from saying *yes...please...*she buried her face in his collar.

The heady mingled scents of warm skin and clean linen did nothing to help, and by the time she'd gathered herself to tell him not to be silly—was it so silly to want to dance?—he was humming a waltz tune as if to himself.

'No,' she said, suddenly panicking as she realised that he was serious. But it was too late. With one arm about her waist and another under her arms supporting her, holding her so that his every move was intensified, telegraphed to her body, he began to turn in wide, slow circles that took them nearer and nearer to the door.

It wasn't dancing—her legs, feet, were not engaged—but every other part of her was suddenly alive and singing and she wanted to laugh out loud.

And then, as they reached the door, he bent. Catching her behind the knees, he scooped her up into his arms.

'You are an amazing dancer, Miss Lang,' he said, 'and I can't wait to tango with you.'

'Not without a rose between your teeth,' she said, a little breathlessly, as if she'd been doing all the work for both of them instead of the other way around.

'Not without a rose,' he agreed. 'And a lot more time.' Then, with a totally unnecessary, 'Hold on,' he carried her through the front door and into the fresh morning sunlight.

That he'd never doubted he'd get his own way was evident from the fact that he'd left it wedged open.

Definitely arrogant, she thought.

But it demonstrated his capacity for forward thinking and meant that he could proceed without, hands full, having to ask her to open it for him. Which also suggested that he'd anticipated resistance.

Arrogant, but smart.

She just hoped that he hadn't worn himself out with that dance. Because the steps up to the footpath were steep and she wasn't exactly a featherweight. As if to confirm her thoughts, his shoulders bunched beneath her hands as he began to climb. The cords on his neck tightened, and against her cheek his pulse quickened—but couldn't begin to match the rapid beat of her own.

And then, as they reached street level—strangely different from this higher vantage point—she saw their local traffic warden open the door of a vintage Bentley. At which point she forgot everything else.

Gleaming silver, it had voluptuous curves, huge silver headlamps and old-fashioned running boards.

It looked the way a car was meant to look. Substantial, expensive and mouth-wateringly desirable.

While she was still staring, open-mouthed, Sebastian crossed the pavement and, with a, 'Mind your head,' that was breathless enough to prove that he was at least human, lowered her carefully into the front passenger seat.

'Okay?' he asked, continuing to hold her while she lifted herself into position, not letting go until he was sure she was comfortable and safe. 'Do you need cushions?'

'Cushions?'

'To wedge you in?'

He leaned into the back of the car and produced a couple of small cushions, and it occurred to her that he'd been doing his homework. Asking questions.

Realising that Sebastian was still waiting for an answer, Matty said, 'Yes. Thank you.' But avoided looking at him while she tucked them around her.

'Old?' she asked, when she was done and he'd finally let go of her and reached across to fasten the seat belt. Already feeling cold, bereft, where his hands had been, she looked around at the luxurious fittings, running her hands appreciatively over the soft leather upholstery as if all she was thinking about was the car. Finally, when he said nothing, she looked up at him. 'This is your idea of an "old" car?'

Actually, it was a great deal easier to concentrate on the car than think about what had just happened. About the way her heart was racing. About the way she'd responded to his closeness. Was still responding to his chin, so close that all she'd have to do was push out her lips to feel the faint stubble, taste him with the tip of her tongue.

Where were such thoughts coming from?

'It is old,' he said. 'Older than me.'

'And you're positively ancient, of course.'

'I'm in my prime,' he assured her, and turned to look at her so that it wasn't his chin that was close enough to kiss but his mouth.

There was nowhere she could go, escape, and for a moment, expecting him to steal another kiss, she stopped breathing, wanting him to take that and more even while she mocked herself for allowing pathetic need to override every scrap of common sense.

'But then,' he continued, 'I'm not a car.' And kept that tiny space between them.

Which was good. Excellent, in fact.

'When you said you'd borrowed a car from your family,' she said, doing her best to organise her tongue and teeth so that she could talk naturally, 'I imagined something less...opulent. If this is a spare, what the heck does your family use to do the weekly shop?'

'You're impressed?' His smile was wry. 'I've finally managed to impress you?'

'The car has impressed me,' she said, waving him away. 'For goodness' sake, Sebastian, leave the seat belt to me. I'm not entirely helpless.'

'Spoilsport,' he said. And then, when it was the last thing she was expecting, he leaned that fraction closer and kissed her again.

CHAPTER NINE

OH, IT was brief. Over in a heartbeat. Pretty much like a lightning strike.

The kiss was light—his mouth in contact with hers, no tongues, nothing sensual—but the energy behind it seemed to pin her to the seat. Which was plainly ridiculous because honestly, if you analysed it, broke it down into its constituent parts, it had to be just about the tamest kiss in the entire world.

He'd just taken her by surprise, that was all. Or maybe it was because it was such an age since a man had kissed her on anything other than the cheek that the effect when Sebastian did it was like drinking a glass of champagne on an empty stomach.

Asking for trouble.

'All right, sir?'

He smiled at her, just for a moment, as if to say, *You see? I know exactly what you want...* before straightening to turn to the traffic warden who was still holding the door.

'Couldn't be better,' he said. 'Just one more minute while I collect Matty's wheelchair?'

'No problem.'

No problem for him.

Sebastian clearly had the neighbourhood traffic warden in the palm of his hand: waiting beside his illegally parked car to give it authority, even opening the door for him.

Now that was *impressive*.

'Don't forget my bag,' Matty called after him, as she

133

snapped home the seat belt fastening with rather more force than it actually required. 'It's on the sofa. And make sure you lock the front door.'

Then, realising that she sounded like a nagging wife, Matty snapped her mouth shut.

'You should get your friend a "Disabled" badge for his car, Matty,' the traffic warden said, staring after him. 'If he's going to be driving you about on a regular basis. I gave him a ticket the other day. If I'd known he was a friend of yours, I'd have come and given you a knock.'

'Don't stress yourself, Sue. This is just a one-off. A business thing.'

'Oh, right. Well,' she said, with a grin, 'nice work if you can get it.' And, with a nod to Sebastian, she moved off along the pavement.

'Is this the one?' he asked, handing Matty a bag. On being assured that it was, he shut the car door, stowed her chair with a commendable lack of fuss, and then climbed behind the wheel. Before she could open her mouth he said, 'Yes, I did.'

'What?' she protested. 'I didn't say a word.'

He started the car and, having checked behind, pulled out into the traffic. 'Yes, I made sure that your front door was securely locked.'

'I wasn't going to ask you that,' she said, lying through her teeth.

'Oh? What were you going to ask?'

'Nothing!'

'I believe you,' he said, reaching out and ruffling her hair. 'This is cute.'

She'd rushed out early yesterday and had it restyled in a feathery, gamine cut before Fran saw what she'd done. There would have been no fooling her with nonsense about thinking she could do it herself. Fran knew too much. It had worked out rather well, and the stylist had talked her into highlights to lighten the whole effect.

'Men aren't supposed to notice stuff like that.'

'Really? No one ever told me. But I'm a bit concerned about what you're going to do with your hands now.'

'My hands?' She held them out in front her, wondering if purple nail polish was a little ridiculous on anyone whose age didn't end with 'teen'.

'You always fiddle with your curls. What'll you do now they've gone?'

'I'm sure I'll think of something,' she said, giving him the coolest look she could summon up.

He grinned. 'Why don't you sort out some music in the meantime?' he suggested. 'There are CDs in the glove-box.'

She continued to look at him for a few more seconds, hoping to imply that strangling him was a lot more tempting, but he seemed intent on the road—which was a very good thing she reminded herself.

Now he'd waltzed her away from her chair, she was totally in his hands—a fact she'd managed to forget in the emotional high of being held in his arms like an ordinary woman.

She'd never even intended to go with him, reasoning that there wasn't the slightest need. But Blanche had phoned with a dozen queries relayed from the software engineer. Sebastian hadn't been in the office, and no one knew where he was, and Matty had begun to worry that the whole scheme might fall apart. And it was probably all her fault. Weeping and making a fuss...

And then there had been the artwork for the rest of the merchandise for the alphabet range. Wrapping paper, the nursery frieze, and a dozen other ideas that she'd finally

had to take to the office herself, to make sure that Blanche
had everything ready in time.

It had seemed obvious that Sebastian was regretting his
decision to try and bail the company out, and in the end,
despite his request to keep her Saturday free, she'd been
the one who'd had to call him and check what time they'd
be leaving.

It had only been after she'd spoken to him that she'd
begun to get the feeling that somehow she'd been had.
That he'd deliberately made her do the chasing.

Which was plainly ridiculous.

But even if it wasn't, it would have been okay. She'd
had the whole thing organised. She was going to drive
herself. That way she'd be in control and could dictate
her own timetable—leave without Sebastian any time she
wanted.

And then, in a rush of sensory intoxication, she'd forgotten every particle of common sense.

She did her best to smother the sudden rush of something very like panic that swamped her, but she must have
made some sound because he glanced at her.

'Problem?'

'No,' she managed. Then, because that wasn't true,
'Actually, yes.'

'Do you want me to pull over? What can I do?' He
didn't wait for her to answer, but eased into the kerb,
ignoring a barrage of 'No Waiting' signs.

'You can't stop here!'

'I've just done it. Tell me what's wrong.'

'I'm sorry.' He seemed genuinely concerned, and that
just made it worse. This wasn't his fault. Well, it was, but
not in a bad way. 'I really should have used my own car.'

'Is my driving really that bad?' he enquired. 'I thought
I'd adjusted to driving on the left pretty well.'

'No!' It was so difficult. 'No. It's not you, Sebastian. It's me.'

He thought about it for a moment, then said, 'No. Sorry, you're going to have to explain that.'

'This way, without my chair, I have no control over what happens to me.' She looked at him, trying to make him understand, trying to get him to feel what she was feeling. Then she shook her head. 'For everything I want, everything I need, I'm going to have to rely on you—and I don't know you well enough for that.'

'No, you don't. But I'm doing my best to remedy that,' he said, very gently. 'I thought we were beginning to get somewhere.'

His voice was pure temptation, but this time she resisted.

She shook her head. 'Please don't make this any more difficult than it needs to be. You know that it can't ever be like that.'

'You're scared?' he asked.

'No!' She shook her head. But then, because she didn't want to lie, because she really wanted him to see, 'Yes.' Then, more emphatically, 'Actually, I'm scared to death.' And then, because it was important he understood, she reached out and covered his hand where it lay, lightly resting on the steering wheel. 'I know you'd never do anything to deliberately hurt me, Sebastian. You just haven't thought this through.'

'I've been thinking of precious little else for the last couple of days. Whatever you want, whatever you need, Matty, you dictate the pace. Would you really be happier if I took you home?'

Noooo! But then her happiness wasn't at issue here.

'Just tell me, Matty. I know I railroaded you into travelling with me. I was just thinking of myself, and I'm sorry. I won't do it again. If you'd rather we used your car, so that you feel in control, I can live with that.'

'You're prepared to take me all the way home and swap vehicles?'

'I don't want you to feel uncomfortable,' he said. 'I hoped today would be fun. About new beginnings for both of us. I don't seem to have made a very good start.'

Actually, she couldn't remember when a day had started so well, but that wasn't what he was talking about. His new beginnings were for the company, and she needed to remember that.

To concentrate on that.

'Your call, Matty,' he prompted.

'Actually,' she said, 'I think we'd better move or we're going to be late. And you'll get another parking ticket.'

'Which way? Forward or back?' he persisted, making her say the word out loud.

'Forward,' she said, trying not to hesitate, wanting to sound certain even if she didn't feel it. 'Life's too short to waste it retracing your steps. Next time just…just listen. Okay?'

And, to indicate that the discussion was over, she leaned forward to look through the music he'd brought with him. For a moment he didn't move, just continued to look at her, but she concentrated on the CDs and finally he pulled back into the traffic and they continued their journey.

Forward.

She'd try to protect him. To be his friend. To send him away before the novelty of her difference wore off and he remembered that he had a real life back in New York. Clearly, since playing hard to get wasn't working, she needed a different approach. Would he stick around a clingy, needy, demanding female?

Her hands were shaking slightly as she slotted one of her favourite albums into the CD-player, and, with Sinatra softly inviting her to fly him to the moon, it occurred to her that something was wrong.

'Was it wise to have a modern CD-player installed in a vintage showpiece car like this?' she asked. 'Doesn't it affect the value?'

'I don't know,' he said. 'And it doesn't matter because no one is going to sell it. It's been in the family since my grandfather bought it, and it's just a car—something to get us from A to B—not a museum piece. Besides,' he said, glancing at her, 'it was a real pain having to keep pulling over to wind up the gramophone.'

'There was a wind-up gramophone...?'

Then she caught the tilt of his lips, the nascent grin, and she realised just how tense she must be, how screwed up with keeping her emotions in check, to have missed such a blatant leg-pull.

'Not fair,' she complained. 'I'm the one who does the teasing.' But she was laughing.

The grin widened. 'I'm a quick study.'

And with that the tension evaporated, and, wrapped in the comfort of the huge leather seat, she decided to stop worrying about protecting them both from the future and enjoy the present—enjoy travelling in the kind of car that turned heads. Enjoy being looked at with envy, for a change, instead of pity.

And whatever else happened today, or in the rest of her life, she'd have Sebastian to thank for that.

'Tell me about New York?' she asked.

Sebastian glanced at Matty. She'd finally stopped hunting for the missing curl and a smile had softened her lips.

Relieved, he said, 'You've never been there?'

'No. I had plans...'

Her voice faltered. She lifted her hands in a gesture that suggested he could see for himself why she'd had to shelve them. Worse, the smile disappeared.

'There's nothing to stop you going any time you want,' he said, in an attempt to salvage that momentary feeling he'd experienced that they were together, two people on an adventure.

He knew a lot about her, but there were still minefields lying in wait, ready to blow up in his face at the first careless word. While Fran had been prepared to offer him practical advice, she hadn't been about to gossip.

He needed to get Matty to open up, talk to him about herself, tell her what her dreams had been before the accident so that he could show her that they could...most of them...still be achieved.

'Plans can be remade,' he assured her. 'All it takes is a little organisation.'

'I know. And I'll do it one day. Soon, if your wheeze with the cards makes me rich.'

'You'll love it,' he said, and just about managed to hold back on an offer to take her there. He didn't want her ducking back behind that self-protective disguise she wore like a shield. The next time she asked him if he wanted to fool around in the bushes he didn't want her to be kidding. He wanted her to mean it. 'It's so full of energy, life.'

'Where do you live?'

He recognised the ploy. Get him to talk so that she didn't have to. Fine, he thought. It was a start. And he told her about his loft apartment, his job, his life, responding easily to prompts as she teased the details out of him. The weekends in the mountains. Summer trips to Cape Cod. She was such a good listener, so easy to talk to, that he'd forgotten that he was supposed to be drawing *her* out. Didn't see the elephant trap yawning at his feet until she asked, 'So, who do you take with you on these trips? I don't see you being short of company.'

'No?' It occurred to him that he'd been short of that for a long time. Not dates, but the kind of woman a man could talk to. 'I just take along whoever I happen to be dating at the time. To be honest it doesn't matter that much who it is.'

'That's not exactly…'

'What?' Then, when she didn't answer, 'Gentlemanly? Probably not.'

'I was going to say, kind.'

'I prefer to date the kind of women who don't expect kindness. It's less complicated.'

'We all hope for kindness, Sebastian,' Matty said, making him feel as if she'd just opened the door onto his world and found—despite his powerful job and high-flying lifestyle—that it was empty.

'There's no one special?' she pressed.

'No, Matty.'

They'd left the main road and had been driving down a long estate road for the last mile or so.

In the distance, his parents' home could be glimpsed through the tress, but long before they reached it he turned through a gate and into the paved yard that fronted the converted stable block that Josh used as his private workshop.

He switched off the engine, sat there for a moment longer, and then, because at some point he had to tell her about Helena, he said, 'I tried "special" once. It didn't work out.'

She'd known. When he'd talked about meeting the right person, she'd known then that he'd had someone he loved.

Matty felt a jangle of emotions. Jealousy, pity. A mixture of wanting to put her arms around him and tell him that they'd all been there and a furious urge to shake him and ask him what he expected if he treated women like the latest piece of technology. Something to be replaced the minute a new model came along.

She took a slow breath and did neither. 'You were married?' she asked, with what she hoped sounded like polite interest. After all, she'd already acknowledged to herself that a man of his age must have been in love once or twice. It followed that he would almost certainly have been married.

'I came close,' he admitted, 'but I didn't quite make it as far as the altar.'

'Oh?' Was that relief? She should not be feeling relief! 'How close to not quite?' she asked.

'Close enough. The church had been booked. The lovely bride had spent hours writing the invitations...' which explained why he knew so much about that '...and the banns had been called.'

'*That* close.'

'It was all very messy.'

She wasn't thinking about the mess of unravelling all that planning, just that the woman he'd loved had changed her mind at the last minute, and without thinking she put out a hand again and covered his where it still lay on the steering wheel. 'I'm so sorry.'

He glanced at her then, a wry smile twisting his mouth. 'Don't waste your pity on me, Matty. I'm afraid I just wasn't the man Helena thought I was.'

Helena.

Matty could imagine her. Tall, with that glossy, dark blonde English hair and finishing school perfection a man like Sebastian would look for in a wife.

'That's when you left London? Went to America?'

'Yes, but I'd already been offered the job. It was when I told her what I wanted to do, how I saw my future, that it became apparent how very different our aspirations were. I thought she knew me. I thought I knew her. It seems we were both wrong.'

'She called it off?'

'No, Matty. I did.'

Despite the sun streaming in through the open car window, she shivered.

That it had never occurred to her that he would have done such a thing demonstrated just how much she already cared for him. Believed in him. The danger she was in.

'The job meant that much to you?' she asked, her voice even.

'It wasn't anything to do with the job.'

'Then, I don't—'

'Seb!' The stable door was flung open and a giant of a man strode out to meet them.

Understand, she thought.

Or maybe she did.

If he'd walked away from a woman he'd loved enough to ask him to marry him, maybe he didn't believe he deserved a second chance. It would explain why he hadn't sought another caring relationship. That desolate emptiness she'd sensed at his core.

And serve to remind her just how important it was to protect herself from caring for him.

'Are you going to sit there all day?' Josh asked, when neither of them made a move. 'Come on, everything's set up and ready for you.' And with a big smile he opened the passenger door. 'You must be the talented Matty,' he said, offering his hand. 'Bea will be so relieved to have someone sensible to talk to at lunch.'

'Lunch?' Sebastian said quickly. 'No, Josh, I've made plans—'

'She insisted, dear boy. Been slaving over a hot stove all morning. My life won't be worth living if I let the pair of you escape unfed.'

'It must be a family thing,' Matty said sympathetically as she took his hand, trying not to wonder what plans... 'Sebastian seems to have something of an obsession about feeding people, too. He just won't take no for—'

'Matty,' Sebastian interrupted, 'this is Josh. Be kind to him, the poor devil is married to my sister.'

'So I gathered,' she said, not missing the fact that he didn't want her to share his eagerness to press lunch on her with his family. He probably didn't want them knowing he was having X-rated thoughts about a woman in a wheelchair. She actually understood. She just wished it didn't hurt so much. 'Which one?' she asked, reaching deep for the careless edge that so usefully distracted the world from feeling sorry for her. 'Bossy, Pushy or Lippy?'

Josh grinned broadly. 'Bossy, without a doubt,' he said. 'But a word to the wise: she'll take anything from her baby brother, but for some reason she expects the rest of us to call her Beatrice—or, on a good day, Bea.'

'I'll try and remember that.' Then, 'Is today a good day?'

He just laughed, keeping hold of her hand, expecting her to lean on him as she climbed out. But before she could explain Sebastian said, 'Leave that to me, Josh. Matty needs her chair.'

'Chair?'

'Wheelchair,' Matty elaborated, fishing in her bag. 'Sebastian's on a steep learning curve, so we may be some time. Do you want to take the disk with the final updates to be going on with?' she said, fishing it out of her bag and handing it to him.

'Oh, right,' he said. 'Well, I'll, um, give it to the boy wonder.'

Sebastian brought the wheelchair around to the front of the car. 'Okay, troublemaker, shall I just pick you up and put you in this, or do you want to show off?'

'Well, let me think about that for a minute,' she said.

He glanced at his watch and said, 'One minute, then you're mine.'

'In your dreams.'

'Time's running out,' he said, leaning into the car, releasing her seat belt and putting his arms around her waist.

Oh, yes...

'You know, this usually isn't a problem. When I'm in my own car all I have to do is operate the lift.'

'I hear you. But, since that isn't going to happen, why don't you just put your arms around my neck and leave the rest to me?'

Because temptation could become a habit. Her arms positively tingled with the desire to let him have his way, to indulge her senses with the softness of his hair, the warmth of his skin as she linked her fingers behind his neck.

A bad habit...

'Because I don't need you to carry me around as if I'm a baby,' she told him. 'And because you should take better care of your back.'

Oh, good grief, he was so close, and that teasing smile of his was an unfair advantage. If he didn't move right now...

'Just take my bag and leave the chair beside me. I can manage perfectly well on my own.' And, because she wasn't convinced that lightning couldn't strike twice in the same place, she gave him a little push just to show him that she meant it.

For a moment he looked as if he'd give her an argument, but then he did exactly as she asked.

No kiss.

Right. Well, he'd said he was a quick study and that was good.

'Do you need me to stay?'

He'd said 'need', not want, she noticed.

'No. Thank you.' Not totally true. She'd have welcomed a safe pair of hands within catching distance. She did this occasionally when she went out with Fran and the children, but her cousin, while pretending to leave her to it, always found some excuse to stay close. Sebastian just nodded and, taking her at her word, turned to follow Josh.

Demonstrating his listening skills? Or already losing interest in the novelty of a woman who couldn't keep up?

Well, fine. She'd been pushing him away from the beginning. Told him the very worst of herself—stuff that she'd never shared with another soul. Not even Fran.

He was the one who kept coming back.

It had been pride that had rejected his help and pride that kept her focussed. If she misjudged the move and landed on her rear she'd never hear the last of it. And the hurt to her pride from having to call for help would be more painful than any fall.

Using her upper body strength, she carefully judged the distance and manoeuvred herself from the car into her chair. Having paused for breath, she then sorted out her legs and backed away from the car so that she could close the door and whizz into the office with the careless insouciance of someone who did that all the time.

Only when she'd shut it did she realise that Sebastian

had gone nowhere, but had stayed close enough to come to her aid if necessary.

'You are amazing,' he said, before she could think of some caustic remark involving babysitters. Instead warmth flooded through her, bringing her ridiculously close to tears. She didn't deserve his kindness. Didn't want it.

'It's nothing,' she said brusquely.

'Sure. I saw. Come and see what Josh and Danny have done.'

CHAPTER TEN

MATTY spent the next hour working with Danny, the pale, skinny youth who'd worked miracles with the software in no time flat, and between them they ironed out the last minor bugs while Sebastian and Josh worked on costs.

'You're pretty nifty with a computer,' Danny said, which she sensed was high praise. 'If I'd had you here earlier in the week this would have been done days ago.'

'Matty had more important things to do, Danny,' Sebastian said, making her feel guilty. He had asked her to come with him, but she'd been more concerned about protecting herself than getting the system right. 'How long will you be? Bea just phoned across to say that lunch is ready.'

Danny shook his head. 'You go ahead. I need to give the system a thorough workout if you insist on taking it with you this afternoon.'

'Can we send something across?' Matty asked, wishing she could stay with him rather than be faced with the prospect of meeting Sebastian's terrifying sister.

He shook his head, engrossed in what he was doing, and they left him to it and joined Bea for a kitchen lunch.

She and Josh lived in a large cottage just behind the stables, with their two teenaged daughters and numerous dogs.

Far from terrifying, Bea was warm in her welcome and, unlike Josh, seemed unsurprised by the wheelchair. And fortunately the downstairs bathroom was a roomy affair in a new extension with doors wide enough for her chair.

'It seemed like a good idea,' she said, when Matty commented on it. 'Josh's father is a bit wobbly on his pins since he had a stroke. Do you need any help?' she asked, so matter-of-factly that if she had it wouldn't have been embarrassing.

'I can manage, thanks.'

Afterwards, while the girls loaded the dishwasher and the men went back to the office to check on progress, Bea suggested she and Matty take their coffee outside, to enjoy the view of the Downs and the sea beyond.

'This is a lovely spot,' Matty said.

'We like it, and the Aged Parents are just up the lane so we can keep an eye on them, whether they think they need us to or not.'

Bea waved in the direction of the large house she'd glimpsed through the trees as they'd arrived. 'Up there.'

Actually, not so much a house, Matty realised, as a small stately home, although there were no signs suggesting it was open to the public. But then, people who kept a spare Bentley in the garage probably didn't need the money.

'I'd suggest Seb take you up there to take a look at the gardens, but it would only be a waste of breath.'

'Oh?'

Bea ignored the opening to gossip and offered Matty a plate of homemade shortbread. 'Help me out with these, will you? The girls have been experimenting with recipes for the cake stall at the summer fête.'

'My cousin has a housekeeper like that, but the results are nowhere near as good. Fortunately the ducks in the park aren't that fussy.'

'Ducks will eat anything, greedy little beggars. You live in London, too?'

'Too? Oh, you mean like Sebastian? Yes.' Then, when

Bea pulled a face, 'Oh, no, really, it's lovely. A garden flat. My cousin Fran and her husband own the house and live in the rest of it. I have to admit that I do have a hankering to move to the country, though.'

'Most people who live in the city seem to. Of course they're usually seeing it on a day like this. It isn't nearly as pretty in the middle of winter with mud up to the back axles, a gale dislodging the roof tiles and a ten-mile drive to buy a pint of milk if you run out.'

'I lived in the country until I went to college,' said Matty, trying to ignore the suspicion that the axles in question were the ones attached to her wheelchair. 'I do have a fair grasp of the downside.'

Bea nodded, evidently accepting that she knew what she was talking about. 'Do you drive?'

This wasn't so much a conversation, Matty realised, as an interrogation, and if Sebastian's sisters treated all the women he knew like this she began to have some sympathy with his view of them.

'Yes, I drive,' she said. 'I have my own specially adapted car. I had intended to use it today, but Sebastian kidnapped me.'

She'd hoped to make Beatrice laugh. Distract her from the inquisition. Nothing doing.

'It's hopeless living in the country if you don't drive,' she said. 'Especially if you've got special needs.'

'It's not much fun living *anywhere* with special needs if you don't drive.' Or can't afford the high cost of an adapted car. Maybe she should be concentrating on stashing something away for the time when it needed replacing, rather than fantasising about a cottage in the country.

'How did you meet?'

The last time she'd been questioned like this, Matty decided, was when she'd applied for a hotly contended

place at art college. Then she'd had no choice but submit.
Now she could, if she wanted to, tell Bea to mind her
own business. But she probably thought it *was* her business if her little brother had got himself tangled up with
a paraplegic female who was going to cause him nothing
but grief.

Her recent recollection of Matthew's mother, sobbing
as she'd thanked her for letting her son go, was a pretty
fair indication of the way any man's family was likely to
respond to such an attachment, and in Bea's place she'd
want to know what was going on, too.

The answer, of course, had to be absolutely nothing.
Not quite true. His kisses suggested that, on the contrary,
Sebastian definitely had plans of the 'going on' variety.
And her responses could hardly be described as 'nothing'.

But she was working on it. It would be easier if she
hadn't got so involved with Coronet…

In the meantime, Bea was waiting for an answer. 'My
cousin Fran—the one whose garden flat I live in—was
married last year. She and her husband, Guy, had a blessing recently, and Sebastian came to the reception.'

'Guy? Guy Dymoke? He's married to your cousin?'

'Yes. You know him?'

'Not well. I was already married back then, but I remember him coming to stay occasionally. I got the impression from Seb that his home life wasn't up to much.'

'That is no longer the case,' Matty said, not quite able
to keep the edge from her voice. Bea was not the only
one who was protective of her family. 'But perhaps, since
you know him, we could dispense with the rest of the
interview? I'm sure he'd give me a character reference.'

Bea stared at her for a moment and then gave a shout
of laughter.

'No need, my dear. No need. It's just good to see my

brother with someone who makes him smile. Since Helena—' She stopped, as if realising that she might have said too much.

'He told me about Helena.'

'Ah, then you understand. It changed him terribly. He used to be such fun, but after the break-up he seemed to turn off all…emotion. It was as if he just wanted to put himself out of reach of everyone.'

She understood the fear of commitment, of allowing someone close. But he seemed to extend it to his family…

'That's why, when Louise phoned and told me about you—'

'Louise?'

'She's our oldest sister. The brainy one. There's Louise, Penny—she lives in France—and me, and bringing up the rear by some distance is Mother's little slip-up— Sebastian.'

Louise, Penny and Beatrice.

Lippy, Pushy and Bossy…

Oh, very funny.

'Pain in the buttocks he might have been as a child, but none of us want to see him get hurt like that ever again, Matty.'

'I'm not going to hurt him,' she said. 'Our relationship is purely business.'

Oh, right. So what about that kiss in the park? There'd been nothing pure about her reaction to that. What about the way he'd waltzed her to the door, held her? She knew how she'd felt, clasped close in his arms, but what about him? What had he been thinking? Feeling?

Whatever it was, she told herself, it had to stop.

'The company engaged me as a consultant,' she said, more to convince herself than Bea. 'I'm just trying to help get Coronet on track so that Sebastian can return to his real life in New York as quickly as possible.'

'And a damn fine job you're making of it,' Sebastian said, reaching between them to take a shortbread from the plate on the table. 'Danny's been printing up a storm. Do you want to come and see?'

Oh, good grief. How long had he been there? What had he heard?

She couldn't even look at Bea.

'We'll both come,' his sister said, clearly not in the least bit embarrassed at being caught discussing his welfare. 'Bring the shortbread, Seb,' she said, leaving them to follow her. 'I'm sure that boy never eats. He just feeds on the light radiating from the computer screen.'

'Yes, ma'am.' Then, when she'd gone, 'Did she give you the third degree?'

'Bea?' Matty swivelled her chair around to follow her, but he stood in front of her, blocking her way. 'I have no idea what you mean.'

'I did warn you,' he said, apparently not convinced. 'B is for Bossy,' he said.

'Yeah, right. I worked out your letter code for myself, thanks. And for your information Bea is not in the least bit bossy. On the contrary, I found her absolutely charming.' She ignored his raised eyebrows. 'And a heck of lot kinder about you than you are about her, I'll have you know.'

'Really? That wasn't me she was referring to as "Mother's little slip-up" then? Age must be mellowing her. Hey, watch out!' he said, as she moved her chair forward, forcing him to step out of the way or risk a sharp crack across the shins from her footrest.

'Show a little respect,' she said.

'You're supposed to be on my side,' he pointed out.

'Really? Who told you that?' When he didn't answer she glanced up sideways at him and discovered that he was grinning. 'Excuse me? Did I say something funny?'

'What? No. Respect. Absolutely. Consider me thoroughly chastised.'

Oh, sure. He looked about as chastised as a dog with two tails.

'So, what did you talk about?' he asked, falling in beside her as she headed back to the office. 'Apart from my somewhat embarrassing arrival on the scene.'

'Embarrassing?'

'For my sisters. Something to do with the thought of their mother having sex, I imagine.'

She tried not to smile. She was cross with him… 'It was a wide-ranging discussion. We talked about the pros and cons of living in the country, the problems with public transport, and your other sisters. I now know, for instance, that Louise—or, as I know her, Lippy—is the brainy one.'

'That's right. She's a professor,' he explained. 'It accounts for the verbal diarrhoea. She never stops telling people what they should think.'

'I couldn't possibly comment on that, although she certainly talks to Bea,' Matty said, glancing up at him. Did he look just a touch uncomfortable? What exactly had he said to Louise about her that had Bea worrying that he was heading for another emotional fall? 'Oh, and we talked about Guy, too. You didn't tell me that Bea knew him.'

'She met him a couple of times when he came home with me. There's a difference.'

'That's true. You've met me a couple of times and you don't know me at all.'

'You can paint,' he said, 'but you can't count. Besides, I'll bet I know a lot more about you than most people.'

Then, 'I also know that you've touched me, made me laugh—'

'It's what I do best,' she said, cutting him off before he could add the rider that she'd made him cry. 'I'm thinking about putting together an act for the Comedy Store.'

'It's not that kind of laughter, Matty, and you know it.' He stopped, folding himself up so that she was looking down at him instead of being forced to look up. He did that, she'd noticed. Thoughtful...

Then he laid his closed hand against her cheek, rubbing his knuckles softly against the down.

'Don't...' she said. 'Please...'

'Don't? Don't tell you that you have genuine empathy, real warmth that touches everyone you meet? Don't tell you that you make me feel...?'

'What?' she demanded, when he appeared to hesitate, the word spilling out before she could lock it up where it could do no harm. She had no right to know what he was feeling. Had no business to be making him feel anything.

He shook his head, smiling. 'Just *feel*, Matty. It's why I won't let you mock yourself. You're too special for that.'

'No.'

She'd thought she could handle this. Thought she could control her feelings. Sebastian would leave sooner or later; she just had to concentrate on Blanche, on Coronet, on her own future. Nothing else was real.

But when he touched her like that something lit up inside her wretched damaged body and she knew she was fooling herself. That she was going to be hurt was inevitable—it had been inevitable from the first moment she'd seen him staring into that glass of warm champagne.

But she wasn't going to hurt him.

'I'm not special, Sebastian. I'm just an ordinary woman who has a bit of a problem with her legs. Don't make me out to be some kind of plaster saint. We both know I'm not that.'

She didn't give him time to answer, but boosted her wheelchair, leaving him behind on the path as she headed towards the office door.

'Come on, let's get this over so that I can go home. I've got a tax return to complete.'

Sebastian didn't argue. He and Josh packed up the hardware, and, after making arrangements for Danny to be in the office on standby, in case of problems on the day the buyer was due, he stowed it all on the rear seat of the Bentley.

Matty, who'd taken the opportunity to freshen up before they left, reappeared from the direction of the house, accompanied by Bea.

'Ready to hit the road?' he asked, looking at her, wishing she wasn't so determined to fight her feelings. So determined to protect him from loving her.

'Absolutely.'

He deliberately turned away, leaving her to get into the car by herself as he shook hands with Josh.

'I can't tell you how much I appreciate all the time and trouble you've put into this,' he said.

'It's for the family. No one wants a mess that will rake up a lot of old gossip. Besides, we've enjoyed doing it. And if it takes off we'll all make money.'

'Well, let's hope that Matty and I can deliver.'

He turned back to Matty, who was now settled in the passenger seat and tucking the cushions about her. He made no comment; he was beginning to get the hang of this and knew that to suggest that she'd done something special would be patronising. He just folded and stowed her chair before climbing in beside her.

'Come and see us again soon, Matty,' Bea said, as he turned the car. 'You should bring her down to the summer fête next week, Seb.'

'Why would I break the habit of a lifetime and come to the summer fête?' he enquired.

'If he won't bring you,' she said to Matty, as he paused to shift gears, 'come on your own. Meet the rest of the family.'

'That's Bea times three,' he warned her. 'Plus my mother.'

'Thank you, Bea,' she replied, pointedly ignoring him. 'I'd love to come if I have time.'

'You don't have to be tactful,' he said, as they headed back towards the road and the somewhat belated continuation of the day he'd planned.

'I meant it.'

'Really?'

'You needn't look so worried. I'll find something to keep me pinned to my drawing board next weekend,' she told him, looking out of the window at the distant view. Anywhere but at him.

Damn, damn, damn…

She thought he didn't want her getting close to his family. Not true. He hadn't wanted to stay to lunch, but only because he hadn't wanted to share more of the precious day with anyone else.

'Shouldn't we have turned the other way?' she asked, as he turned south on the main road.

'Only if we wanted to go back to London. I should probably have made it clear that the only reason I didn't want to stay to lunch with Bea and Josh was because I'd planned something more interesting.'

That, at least, brought a smile to her lips.

'Oh, dear. Another lunch plan ruined. Maybe someone's trying to tell you something. Maybe you should take the hint and give up.'

'I'm not a quitter.'

'No,' she said, 'you're not that. But why didn't you just tell Bea you had other plans?'

'Because she and Josh normally make do with a sandwich at lunchtime. He's busy in his workshop, or down at the business park where the real work gets done. She has a dozen or more committees to keep in order. Believe me, I didn't get that spread when I came by myself earlier in the week.'

'She cooked specially for me?'

'She wanted to make you feel welcome.' Then he shrugged. 'And, of course, she wanted to give you the third degree. It would have been heartless to have disappointed her.' He glanced at her. 'You do keep telling me to be nicer to my sisters.'

'My mistake.' Then, relenting sufficiently to grin at him, 'You might have warned me I was going to be put through an inquisition.'

'I did. You just weren't listening.'

'You talked to Louise about me, didn't you? What is she a professor of?'

He shrugged. 'One of the sciences.'

'Seriously brainy, then?'

'She got the brains; I got the looks—'

'Which branch?' she asked, ignoring his attempt to divert her. 'Physics? Biology?'

He took his time about answering, making a big deal of concentrating while he negotiated a roundabout, but there was no avoiding the question.

'Medicine,' he said.

The car whispered across the Downs baking under the afternoon sun and curving away to a sea that blended so perfectly with the sky it was hard to tell where one ended and the other began.

When Sebastian turned off the main road and down a narrow lane marked 'Private', Matty didn't even bother to point it out, instead reaching for the missing curl, needing something to do with her hands as she worked out what she felt about Sebastian ringing his brainy doctor sister to talk about her. What had he wanted to know? What had Louise told him?

'You're really going to have to let your hair grow again,' he said, after she'd reached for it a third time, snatching her hand away when he grinned.

Matty didn't answer. She simply tucked her hands beneath her legs.

'Why did you cut it?'

He'd taken his time about asking the question, but she'd known it would come and was ready for it now.

'I used to have really long hair,' she said. 'I used to spend so much time on it. Straightening it, streaking it pink, blue, gold, sometimes all three at the same time, to match my mood.'

She still expected to see it every time she looked in the mirror...

'I have pictures somewhere,' she said. 'Pictures of me dancing, with my hair flying out around me. Pictures of me lying on a beach. Pictures of me on bicycle, cleaning my car, sailing—'

The car had stopped moving, and she stopped, too. He had brought her to a small sandy cove, hemmed in by chalk cliffs. There was a small stone cottage nestled in the lee of the one standing out against the prevailing weather. It had its own wooden dock and a boathouse, with a ramp to launch a dinghy into the water.

The tide was only halfway in and there were exposed rock pools—the kind that kids loved to poke about in. The kind where the water got really warm on a day like today, where you could sit and dangle your toes...

'Now I just sit on the sidelines and watch,' she said.

'You don't have to. Life hasn't stopped, Matty.'

'No,' she said, remembering the last time she'd been on a beach. Walking along the water's edge, feeling the wet sand squeezing between her toes, her fingers entwined in those of the man she'd thought she was going to spend her whole life with. 'It hasn't stopped, but it has changed.' She looked at him then. 'I'm sure Louise laid it all out in black and white for you. What I can't do. What I have to do. The daily exercise routine to keep the muscles that work fit enough to take up the strain for those that don't. The medication. You don't want to be around me if I don't take my medication,' she told him.

'What's the big deal about regular exercise? And Josh is diabetic. He has to inject insulin every day, but you don't hear him whining about it.'

She let out a puff of outraged breath. How dared he suggest for one minute that she whined?

'And for your information,' he went on calmly, 'no, I didn't ask my sister to lay out your problems for me. I just asked her where I could find the information for myself and she directed me to a couple of websites.'

'Oh.' Then, 'Why?' He looked at her, and that was all she needed by way of answer. 'Oh, right. We've had the dance, and you've fed me more than once, so now you think it's about time I delivered with the fooling around in the bushes deal. Have I got it right? What is it, Sebastian? Does the wheelchair turn you on? You wouldn't be alone, you know. Some men just love a helpless woman…'

It was a shocking, hateful thing to say. But without warning everything seemed to have got out of hand. She didn't want to be in this beautiful place with him, pretending that all was right with the world. It wasn't, and if by mocking him, hurting him, she could make him stop whatever it was he thought he was doing, drive him away—well, she'd done it before and she could do it again.

But he didn't look shocked, or hurt. His eyes were dark with some quite different emotion as he leaned forward, tugged her hand free, kissed the palm and then said, 'It's not the wheelchair, it's you. You turn me on, Matty.'

And he carried her hand to his groin, to show her exactly how much.

She almost yelped as she felt how hard he was. Opened her mouth to say something. Closed it again because she couldn't actually think of anything to say.

And finally Sebastian smiled. 'Well, what do you know? I've actually managed to render you speechless.'

'I…' No, that wasn't right. 'You…'

'Try *we*,' he said, lifting her hand, holding it in his. Then, 'Is swimming part of your exercise routine?'

'Well, yes.' Then, realising what he was suggesting, 'No!'

'I love a decisive woman.'

She turned to look at the sea. 'I swim in the local pool a couple of times a week.'

'Then you swim.'

'It's not the same.'

'No,' he said. 'The pool is safe and tame. Don't you just long to break out? Take a risk or two?'

'I haven't swum in the sea since before the accident,' she protested.

'You haven't been to the sea since before the accident, have you?'

'I...' She couldn't lie to him. 'No. I couldn't face it.'

He reached across to the glove compartment and took out the discarded picture that he'd picked up from her studio floor. 'You already have. It's time to stop punishing yourself, Matty'

'I'm not!' He said nothing and she repeated the words. 'I'm not punishing myself!'

'Then let your hair grow long,' he said. 'Stop denying that you're a whole woman.'

'If you knew why I cut my hair, why did you ask?'

'I wanted to be sure that you knew, too. And now that we've got that out of the way we'll go for that swim.'

'Why should I?' she demanded, with a last stab at resistance.

He leaned across and touched her cheek, turning her face until she was looking directly at him. 'Because you want to more than anything in the world.' There was no teasing now. His eyes were grave. 'Am I wrong?'

She should tell him that he was, got as far as opening her mouth to say so, but she just couldn't make her mouth say the words. He was right. She'd loved to swim in the sea. Feel the suck of the water around her. It was alive, moving...

But it was the thought of being in the water with him that was so special. No—completely irresistible.

Apparently satisfied by her silence, Sebastian climbed out of the car, got out her wheelchair and, without bothering to ask, lifted her out of the car and placed her gently into it.

'This is ridiculous, Sebastian. I haven't got a costume with me.'

'That's all right,' he said, reverting to teasing now that he'd got his way. 'Neither have I. But don't worry. You can keep your underwear on if you're shy. Of course that's just delaying the inevitable. I won't be responsible for you sitting around in wet things, so you'll have to take it off when you come out of the water.'

She swallowed. There had to be a hundred reasons why this was a bad idea. Tomorrow, for instance, when she'd have to face herself in the mirror. Next week, when she'd have to face Sebastian in a business setting and pretend that none of this had happened.

But somehow she couldn't actually begin to care that much about tomorrow when she felt so suddenly alive today.

'What about the people who live in the cottage?' she asked. 'Won't they object to a couple of total strangers swimming naked in their private bay?'

Which more or less disposed of the underwear question.

'The cottage is empty.' And, making a broad gesture that took in their surroundings while never taking his eyes of her, he said, 'This is all ours.'

She looked at the sea, a shimmering tempting blue, then back at Sebastian. His eyes were the same colour. They seemed to be challenging her, to be saying, *I dare you...*

If the sun hadn't been beating down on her, she'd still have been hot. 'Okay,' she said, before she could lose her nerve. 'So how are we going to do this?'

'Let's get down to the boathouse. Once we're there, I'll take care of the rest.'

She led the way onto the deck at the side of the boathouse briskly enough, but then, as she realised what she was about to do, her confidence began to ebb away.

She was going to take her clothes off in front of Sebastian—not in the throes of passion, not in the dark, but in the brassy light of the July sun. No shadow, no hiding place.

Her doubt must have been evident, because he reached out, touched her cheek and said, 'Trust me, Matty...'

And instead of thinking, Why? she thought, Why not? What is the worst thing that could happen?

That Sebastian would take one look at her body and instantly wish he'd chosen some other way to spend the afternoon?

Would that be her problem, or his?

Not one that was bothering him, she decided, as he pulled his shirt over his head and dropped it on the deck.

'This is going to be fun.'

Fun?

Trust me... This is going to be fun.

She'd been stressing about what he'd think of her boobs, or whether her legs would be too thin, when the only thing on his mind was having fun.

'Of course it is,' she said, grinning broadly. It already was, she realised, looking at his wide, well-muscled shoulders. His lightly tanned skin gleamed gold in the sun, making her fingers itch to paint him naked, regret that she hadn't brought a camera with her.

If she'd known he was bringing her to the sea she'd have picked up the little digital job that Fran had given her for her birthday.

But then if she'd known he was bringing her to the sea she'd have locked herself inside her flat and nothing would have got her into his car.

CHAPTER ELEVEN

SEBASTIAN kicked off his shoes, peeled off his socks and added them to the pile, then unbuckled his belt and dropped his jeans, stepping out of them as if it was the most natural thing in the world. At which point Matty realised she'd stopped breathing some time ago.

He turned to face her, the soft grey boxers straining tight across his hips, leaving little to the imagination.

Finally she'd met a man prepared to call her bluff, she thought. A man who would dare her to match her bold words with deeds.

'Need a hand?' he asked.

'Um...'

Taking that as a yes, he knelt in front of her and removed the ballet pump shoes she was wearing.

'You've painted your toenails too,' he said, and she was glad she'd made the effort. 'They're very...purple.'

'I used to match my nails to the streaks in my hair,' she told him.

'So why don't you do it now? No complaints—the blonde highlights look great—but I see you as a woman who likes to make an impact.'

'We all have to grow up.'

'That's no excuse to get boring.'

'Boring!'

'Oh, dear. I appeared to have touched another of those hot buttons of yours,' he said, grinning broadly.

'Excuse me,' she said, fists on hips, 'but would someone "boring" be stripping off and swimming naked in the sea?'

'Oh, is that what you're doing? And I thought you were just sitting there admiring the view.'

'There's a lot to admire,' she said, then blushed.

'If that's the case, then why don't you just sit back and enjoy it?' he said. 'Leave all the work to me.' Without waiting for an answer, he began to unbutton the short-sleeved shirt she was wearing loose over a matching ankle length skirt.

He was going to undress her?

'What are you doing?' she demanded.

'I told you I'd take care of the details,' he said. 'I meant it.' He paused, his hands resting lightly between her breasts, and looked up. 'Do you have a problem with that?'

With a tingle of anticipation rippling through her, and his 'boring' taunt still ringing in her ears, she gave a care-less wave, although she couldn't quite meet his gaze as she said, 'No. Carry on.'

Actually, it came out as more of a squeak, but she had to admit there was absolutely nothing boring about Sebastian.

And suddenly, as the buttons were slipped from the buttonholes one at a time, it seemed that getting out of her clothes was the easiest thing in the world. Of course he was very good at it. He had her shirt off before she had time to worry about it.

'Now, that's what I call user-friendly,' he said, looking at her bra with appreciation. 'A front-opening bra.'

Matty's only thoughts were relief that she was wearing something sexy, something worthy of the moment.

'You like it?'

'It's much too pretty to risk submerging in seawater,' he said, unhooking it.

Actually, she was fairly sure that his fingers were trembling a little as he did that. His Adam's apple certainly bobbed up and down a couple of times in quick succession, which was deeply satisfying.

'This exercise routine you do,' he said, a touch hoarsely, 'I want you to know that it really works...'

Not that cool, then.

Then, quickly getting to his feet, he leaned forward, and she needed no prompting to put her arms around his neck so that he could lift her as he slid his hands under the elasticated waistband of her skirt. For a moment her breasts brushed against him, the light spattering of hair on his chest bringing a shiver to her skin as, with one easy movement, he had her skirt and pants down and she was back in the chair. Only now she was naked.

'Okay?' he asked.

'Only if it's okay to be terrified.'

'Terror is fine. Boredom is the killer,' he said. And he shucked off his boxers, giving her a brief, heart-stopping reminder of what exactly it was that she did to him, before scooping her up and walking carefully down the shallow slipway and into the water.

She was out of her depth and floating. The water was a lot colder than in the local swimming pool, and the initial immersion had shocked her into action. She'd twisted out of Sebastian's arms and taken off, swimming fast across the bay, the strength in her shoulders and arms making up for her useless legs.

Sebastian had easily kept pace with her, swimming on the seaward side, reaching out to steady her when a larger than usual wave caught her by surprise and left her momentarily floundering.

Now she was lying on her back, watching the seagulls soaring over the clifftops, feeling utterly relaxed and at home in the water. As if it were her natural environment.

'Shame about your hair,' Sebastian said, floating at her

side, her hand in his as if to stop her from drifting away from him. 'If you hadn't cut it you could sit on a rock and pretend to be a mermaid.'

'Pretend?' She rolled over, taking him by surprise. 'Who's pretending?' And she pushed him down beneath the water, where they were weightless. Equals.

She kissed his salty lips, his throat, sliding down his body until she was kissing him more intimately, taking him in her mouth, seducing him as if she were truly a wicked mermaid, luring him to his doom.

Time seemed an infinitely elastic affair. She felt powerful, strong. Breathing was forgotten. Mermaids weren't subject to the laws of nature...

And then, somehow, she was plunging back into the air and gasping like a fish. Sebastian's arms were under her arms, holding her up, holding her close against him, and he was kissing her as if he were trying to pour all his strength into her, as if he were giving her the kiss of life, and she drank him in.

Finally Sebastian drew back, looked her in the eyes. 'You do know you scared me half to death?'

'I did?' She grinned, her chest heaving as it sucked in air. 'That really wasn't my intention.'

'How can you hold your breath for that long?'

'I swim lengths under water at the pool. I feel free there.' Then, because she knew that she was the one who dictated what happened next, she said, 'I've never made out in the back of a Bentley. Why don't you take me there so that I can finish what I started?'

'We'll save the Bentley for another time. Right now, I've got something a little more comfortable in mind,' he said, lifting her so that she was lying back in his arms as he swam with her towards the shore. 'And you may have started this, but I think you should know now that in any kind of a contest with a woman I make a point of coming last.'

His feet touched bottom and he carried her up the small beach to the cottage. 'Do you want to open the door?'

'Sebastian! We can't!'

'Relax, we're not breaking and entering. This place is owned by my family.'

'It is?' Actually, that made sense. How else would he know the cottage was here, the bay was here at the end of a road marked 'Private'? 'You leave it unlocked?'

'No, my love. I unlocked the door when I followed you to the boathouse. You were too busy imagining what I'd look like with my kit off to notice. Now, do you want to waste time discussing security, or do you want me to use my mouth for something more interesting?'

She gave a little gasp and he smiled. 'I'll take that as a yes. The door?'

Matty turned the handle and Sebastian shouldered his way in, kicking the door shut behind him. She saw the open-slatted wooden stairs rising to the first floor and thought, He's never going to make it. He didn't even try, but instead crossed the open-plan living room to a room beyond it that was furnished as a bedroom. The bed was freshly made, the cover turned down.

'You came here in the week,' she said. 'You planned this.'

'Guilty as charged,' he said, sitting on the bed, rolling her onto it. And then he was above her, and she saw nothing but his sea-coloured eyes, intent, burning, as he delivered on his promise.

He took his time, kissing her mouth, her eyes, using his hands, his fingers, his tongue on all those sensitive spots that had lain dormant for so long. He breathed kisses onto her breasts, gently as first, then with more urgency, until she was loudly demanding more and the heavy aching need that might have been in her head, but seemed very real, could only be fulfilled in one way.

'Now,' she pleaded. 'I need you now.'

'You're sure?'

For one hideous moment she thought that he was having doubts, that her unmoving lower limbs had turned him off.

'Are you?'

His answer was to kiss her mouth, then hand her the protection he'd had ready. 'Why don't you put this on for me,' he suggested, 'and find out for yourself?'

She hadn't known what to expect. She knew that everything worked, but sex was so much more than tab A fitting into slot B. There were emotions, the deep-seated guilt, a belief that she did not deserve this...

But she was feeling something. Just as she had when he'd first kissed her in the park. The brain making adjustments, compensating, she'd rationalised then. Except that it was so much more than that. And not just for her.

Sebastian waited and waited until she had achieved something she'd thought impossible. But it was his own shattering climax that gave her back her femininity, made her feel like a woman for the first time in three years.

Sebastian lay propped on his elbow remembering, as he watched her sleep, that his first thought on seeing Matty had been that she was nondescript. Mousy.

She opened her eyes.

Except for her lovely amber eyes.

'You're beautiful, Matty,' he said, then kissed her. 'But I think you should seriously consider putting purple streaks in your hair.'

'Right now?' she asked.

'Well, maybe we should eat first.'

'You've had the sex, Sebastian,' she said, smiling. Not

the surface smile with which she kept everyone at bay and behind which she hid her true feelings, but really smiling. 'You don't have to keep plying me with food.'

'That would be true, except that I'd rather like to do it again.'

'I don't want to leave you,' Sebastian said when he delivered her back to her flat on Sunday evening. He kissed her, leaned his forehead against hers and said, 'Come and stay with me.'

Hard as it was to say no, send him away, she forced herself.

They'd stayed at the cottage until Sunday evening, talking, eating the contents of a large cold box that Sebastian had brought with him, swimming, making love. Actually, she'd done most of the talking, but he'd asked all the right questions, so that by the time they'd left the cottage he knew everything there was to know about her. Her fractured family, school, college. It had just spilled out as if a dam had burst.

But now she needed some time to put what had happened into some kind of context. Take a reality check. Take back a little of her life.

And he needed to concentrate on convincing the buyer for the retail chain that Coronet, even without George at its head, was still a vibrant brand.

Blanche had organised a display area in the lobby of the office, laying it out like a shop, with all the new ranges prominently displayed. She stood back, watching while Sebastian walked round, touching things here and there, moving something that obscured part of the alphabet frieze. Wiped an imaginary speck of dust from the computer system set up for the 'print your own' alphabet cards.

'The Botanicals look really good,' he said approvingly,

then glowered at the *Forest Fairies*, who were still there—if not in pride of place any more.

Then he came to a full stop at the sight of the reprints of the first cards the company had ever produced to help out George's art school colleagues.

'What are these doing here?' he demanded.

'I didn't want to tell you until I had the last of the permissions in writing,' Blanche said, her voice calm, but with a smile that suggested cats and cream.

'Permissions?'

'I got in touch with all of them. They were George's friends and they all know what they owed him.'

'And they all just said, "Go ahead, print what you like"?'

'No, I've agreed to limit the number produced, but that's good. It'll stimulate demand. If your man wants to be sure to have some, he'll have to move quickly—especially as I've agreed that at least twenty-five per cent of them will be sold through independent outlets. Half of those are already spoken for.'

'You have been busy. What else have you agreed?'

'To set up a bursary for promising art students in George's name. Actually, that was my idea. The hook. Without exception they agreed that we could use the profits for the fund.'

'Well, that's fine, Blanche, but what's the bottom line? Will we actually make any money?'

'Not as much as on the rest of the range,' she admitted. 'But we're going to be getting the kind of publicity that money can't buy.'

'We are?' Sebastian looked as if he might take issue with that, but Blanche didn't give him the opportunity.

'Especially now that the college has agreed to co-operate, so that next year we'll be producing a range of new "new" artists. I've been promised a feature on that next autumn in one of the Sunday supplements. A piece about George, the company, the first "new" artists and the new "new" artists.'

'Next autumn? Oh, well, great. What can I say? You've done an amazing job, Blanche.'

'Oh, credit where it's due—'

Matty quickly shook her head.

Sebastian, sensing something, turned to look at her. 'I think what Blanche is trying to say, Sebastian, is that this is all down to you. If you hadn't taken the time and trouble to put the company back on track, none of this would have happened.'

'Oh, really? Is that what you were trying to tell me, Blanche?'

'Mmmm.'

'Now it's your turn to do what you do best,' Matty said quickly. 'Go and buy this guy the kind of lunch that will put him in the mood to buy big.'

His face creased in a smile. '*Our* turn, ma'am. You could wear down stone.'

'I still don't believe it,' Sebastian said later, when they were curled up together on Matty's sofa. 'All that stressing and without prompting that guy said he was going to double last year's order for the entire range of *Forest Fairies*.'

'Your face was an absolute picture. I guess blessings upon satellite TV reruns are the order of the day.'

'It would have been helpful if we'd known about that.'

'Nonsense. If you'd known, you wouldn't have put anywhere near as much effort into the new lines.'

'I just wish he'd been more positive about the "print-your-own" alphabet cards.'

'It was always going to be too big a decision for him to make. Actually, I thought it was promising that he was talking about what other lines it could be programmed to produce.'

'You're right, of course. I just wanted it for you.'

She touched her head against his shoulder, acknowledging the fact, and he reached out and put his arm around her.

'They'll probably want to run trials in some of their bigger shops first.'

'Bound to. The reproduction of the original cards was a real winner. Blanche did a great job there, Sebastian.'

'With your help.'

'You'll be getting a note of my fee in due course,' she said, grinning. Then, because it had to be faced, 'At this rate you'll be back in New York before you know it.'

'I'm in no rush.'

'Your life is there, Sebastian. Rescuing Coronet was always just a minor diversion.'

Just as she was a minor diversion.

'I still have to find a buyer for the company. It won't be that easy, but that's okay. It gives me time.'

'Time?'

'To convince you that you should come to New York with me.' Matty thought she must have misheard, but before she could twist her head round to check out his expression he said, 'My apartment is wheelchair-friendly, and you do most of your work over the internet.'

'It is?' She frowned, trying to remember what he'd told her about it. 'What about the spiral stairs to the sleeping loft?'

'I'll put in a lift.'

'But—'

He stopped her with a kiss that went on for so long she forgot what she was going to say. Her silk shirt was on the floor by the time she remembered…

'No…'

He stopped. 'No? You don't want me to take your clothes off?'

'Yes, but...'

'Then everything else can wait. You've got months to come up with all the reasons in the world why you can't possibly leave London. And I've got months to discount them—'

'No, Sebastian, you have to listen—'

'And I will. But not now. All I want to hear you say now is yes.'

She pressed her lips firmly together, refusing to fall for that one.

'Yes, you'll think about it,' he said, grinning. 'Yes, we can go to bed.' The smile faded as he leaned into her, kissed her, then said, very softly, 'Yes...yes...yes...'

Sebastian watched Guy playing with his stepson on a little jungle gym set up on the lawn and tried to analyse his feelings. The one thing he'd never wanted was a son. He'd wondered whether as he got older, or if he met the right woman, he would change. Now he knew it was an irrelevance. It was the woman who mattered. All the rest was in the lap of the gods.

He'd have to talk to Matty about that. It was the one excuse she hadn't made yet. He fancied she was keeping it until last. The big one.

He needed to get in with his feelings first, he realised. It was time to tell her a lot of things. Make it absolutely clear how he felt. But she wasn't here.

Toby spotted him, wriggled down from the climbing frame, and Guy looked up.

'Seb!' Then, 'If you're looking for Matty, you've missed her by about an hour.'

'Any idea when she'll be back?'

'Not until late, I shouldn't think. When I saw her loading up the car she told me you were spending the day in heavy meetings with someone wanting to buy the company. How did it go?'

'It didn't. I decided I'd much rather spend a sunny Saturday with my girl. Loading her car?'

'Easel, drawing stuff. She does these brilliant little portrait sketches of kids—well, you've seen the one of Toby in my office. It seems Bea called and talked her into doing them at the fête.'

'Fête?'

His blood ran cold. She was going to the summer fête in the grounds of his parents' home. An annual event to raise funds for some local need or other. New bell ropes, or repairs to the church roof, or a hut for the Scouts.

'Ask Fran to try and raise her on her mobile, will you? Make some excuse to get her back here.'

'No chance. Even before it became illegal to speak while driving, she never has her phone switched on when she's in the car.'

No. Of course not.

CHAPTER TWELVE

'LOUISE and Penny are up at the Hall with the Aged Parents. Drive me up there,' Bea said, climbing in beside her, 'and we'll get the formalities over with.'

'The formalities?'

'Penny and Louise are keen to meet you.' She must have looked as panic-stricken as she felt, Matty thought, because Bea grinned reassuringly. 'It's okay. I promise you they're nowhere near as bad as Sebastian painted.'

'How…?' Then, when Bea laughed, 'No, of course not. They couldn't possibly be.'

'Once that's over with I'll show you where I've set you up. It's really kind of you to do this—we're always desperate for some new attraction, and I know you're going to be a hit, but don't feel you have to perform non-stop. And use your phone to call me if you need refreshments or rescuing from the gawpers.'

'Gawpers?'

'Everyone will want to meet you. Take a look at the son and heir's new girl.

'I'm not—' she protested. Then, realising she was not convincing anyone, 'They know nothing about me.'

'You've been here. You were with Sebastian. People tend to notice strangers in the country. And they're very quick to put two and two together.'

'They're making five,' she declared.

'They always do. Over here,' Bea said, directing her to the rear of the mini stately home. Then, leaning out of the window, 'Daddy!'

The man who approached the car was tall, distinguished, and undoubtedly Sebastian's father. The likeness was remarkable.

'Daddy,' Bea said rather loudly as she leaned across her to talk through the open window, 'this is Matty. She's a friend of Sebastian's.'

'Delighted to meet you, m'dear. Is Grafton with you?'

Matty glanced at Bea, puzzled, but she just shook her head as if to say *Don't ask* and replied, 'Matty came on her own. I'm just taking her to meet the rest of the females.'

'Penny's gone down to the lake on guard duty.' He looked at Matty and said, 'Some idiot always falls in. Louise is checking up on the first-aiders, and your mother's with that actor chap who's come to open us.'

'Oh, right. Later, then.'

When he'd gone Matty looked at Bea again. 'Who's Grafton?'

Bea shrugged. 'Daddy's a bit old-fashioned. He always calls Seb by his title. It drives him up the wall.'

Title?

'I'm sorry. Did you say title?'

At which point Bea realised that she hadn't a clue and let slip a word that, as the mother of teenage girls, she would normally have kept behind tight lips.

'He hasn't told you, has he?'

'Apparently not.' Matty managed a smile that she was really quite proud of. 'But don't worry. He will.'

The road was murder, clogged with people trying to escape the city for a weekend at the coast. When Sebastian finally arrived at the fête he knew it would be too late to do more than pick up the pieces. Try and convince Matty that it didn't matter.

Not true.

He'd already lost one woman because of a title he didn't want. He should have told Matty then, when he'd told her about Helena. He'd intended to, but then Josh had come to see what was keeping them…

No. No excuses. No lies.

For Matty only the truth would do. The whole truth.

He saw her long before she saw him. She was sketching a fair-haired moppet, chatting as she worked, making the child giggle. Then, as she tore off the sheet and handed it to the little girl's delighted mother, she saw him.

Her smile scarcely wavered before the next child sat on the stool and she carried on, asking her name, putting her at her ease. There were a couple of other people waiting, and when he joined them she looked up, but she wasn't looking at him. She was looking right through him.

'I'm taking a break in half an hour,' she said. 'Why don't you go and do your thing? Rustle up a sandwich and we'll have a little picnic.'

She was smiling, spoke sweetly enough to convince the curious onlookers, but he wasn't fooled for a minute.

'I'll be down by the lake when you're ready.'

There were a couple of children at the water's edge trying to scoop out carp with paper cups. No one seemed to be keeping an eye on the lake and he should probably stop them. Instead he sat on a bench far enough away not to spoil their fun.

After what seemed like a lifetime, Matty rolled to a halt beside him.

He'd spent every second since he'd left London trying to think of something that would make this all right.

Fortunately—because there were no words—she didn't wait, but said, 'I told you everything. Things about me that even Fran doesn't know.' Her voice, normally so warm, was cold, and her words hammered at him like little chips of ice. 'I never told anyone else about the mobile phone. Everyone was so kind. So sympathetic. And I was so ashamed that I couldn't tell them that the accident was entirely my own fault. That I was to blame…'

She looked at him then, and the force of anger she'd been keeping so tightly under control hit him like a blow. Her eyes was blazing. Hot. Bright with tears.

'Matty—'

'I spilled my heart out to you.'

And suddenly it was all absolutely crystal-clear, and he knew exactly how to get her to listen to him.

'Why?' he asked.

'Why?'

'Why did you tell me?' He wasn't being gentle. Gentleness was not the answer now. 'What was it about me that made you want to bare your soul, hmm?'

She swallowed, floundered at his unexpected challenge, and he knew he was right.

'Does it matter?' she asked.

'Of course it matters—or why are you bringing it up now?'

Not cruel to be kind. Cruel to get at the truth.

He'd just handed her the biggest excuse in the world to run away from their future, and she was going to use it and run unless he forced her to face her fear—just as he'd forced her into the sea. She'd broken free then, found something inside herself. Something she'd buried deep. He would have to make her go there again.

'You told me how the accident happened,' he said, 'because you thought it would drive me away.'

'No!'

'Admit it! You wanted me to think as badly of you as you did of yourself.'

'You bastard!'

Well, yes. Obviously. She'd got it in one...

'You told me nothing,' she declared. 'Absolutely nothing. I knew you were a hot-shot banker from New York before I met you. That's all I know now.'

'Is it? Really?'

She didn't answer, but reached for the non-existent curl. He caught her hand, held it.

'You know that's not true.' She tugged at her hand, but he didn't release it. 'It didn't work, Matty, and neither will this. So don't turn this into some major drama just so you can chicken out of confronting the big, frightening decision about our future—about us—and dump the blame at my door.'

Was she listening? Was she hearing him?

'Or do you want to run back to your safe little garden flat with a twice weekly trip to the swimming pool? Do you want to spend the rest of your life making verbal passes at men who stray near your wheelchair—passes that you're too scared to follow up on? Are you a mermaid, or a mouse?'

Her mouth worked, but no sound emerged.

'I love you, Matty. You're a strong, wonderful woman and I want to spend the rest of my life getting to know you. I want you to be my wife.'

'You can't.' She looked up, and this time the tears were pouring down her cheeks. 'You're going to be an earl. You'll want sons...'

'No. I can't do anything about a courtesy title except refuse to use it. But I can and will reject the Earldom. I don't want sons to perpetuate an outdated hierarchy system, Matty.' He was on his knees before her. 'Listen to me. I just want you.'

She shook her head. 'Why didn't you tell me?'

'Go away, Sebastian.' He looked up at the sound of his mother's voice. 'I want to talk to Matty.'

'I can handle this,' he replied coldly.

'I know, but I owe you this. Let me help.' She held herself with the carriage and bearing of everything that she was, but her eyes were begging him. 'Please.'

He raised Matty's hand to his lips, then silently mouthed the words again—*I love you*—before standing up and walking away.

Even as Sebastian walked away from her Matty wanted to call him back. It was just as well that his mother was there.

'May I sit down, Matty?'

Somehow it didn't seem polite to remind her that it was her bench, that she could do anything she wanted, so she just nodded.

'Thank you.' After a moment, his mother said, 'Sebastian should have told you this himself, but I know he won't. He despises me, but he would never betray me. He takes that from my husband. Honour, duty.'

She didn't know what the woman was talking about, but she said, 'Right.'

'I understand from my daughters—Sebastian doesn't speak to me if he can possibly avoid it—that my son loves you. Indeed, I heard him say so with his own lips. Which is why I'm going to tell you what he will not. Sebastian is not my husband's legitimate heir. I had an affair. My marriage was going through a bad patch and I turned to someone I'd known a long time for easy comfort. I'm not making excuses. I despised myself for being so weak. The only comfort was Sebastian.'

'He's not...' Matty was stunned. 'But they're so alike...' Even as she said the words she worked it out for herself. 'George. George was Sebastian's father, wasn't he?'

'Ah, I see you've heard of him. He was my husband's cousin. They were as alike as twins in looks. In temperament...chalk and cheese.'

'Does your husband know?'

'Oh, yes. One of the girls brought mumps home and put an end to his attempts to get an heir several years before Sebastian was born. He was actually quite grateful to George for filling the gap, so to speak. Keeping it in the family is so much tidier. Sebastian seems to have taken the best from both men. His charm and artistic temperament he takes from George. From the man who raised him as his own he's learned honour, and to be faithful unto death.'

Faithful unto death?

'What about Helena?'

'That shallow little trollop? When she found out that Sebastian meant it, really meant it, about not taking the title, she showed her true colours. He begged me to tell her why.'

'You refused?'

'If a title matters more than the man...' She shook her head. 'He didn't see it that way, of course. Love is blind.' She reached out, took her hand, held it for a moment. 'Go with him, Matty. Make him happy. He deserves it.' She stood up, kissed Matty's cheek. 'See if you can persuade him to come home to us for Christmas. I miss him so much.' Then, 'Shall I send him back to you?'

'Give me a while. I need to think.'

In the event she didn't have time to think. One of the children playing at the edge of the water overbalanced and disappeared beneath the water. Without stopping to think, she slipped the brake on her chair and boosted it towards the lake, throwing herself in the water, diving down to grab him as he sank into the murk at the bottom.

'Don't make a fuss. And don't let that cameraman—' There was a flash. 'Nooo! I'm covered in mud and water weeds. I don't want my picture in the local paper.'

'Local? You're kidding. "Viscount's Lover in Lake Rescue" will make the tabloids.' Sebastian grinned. 'Or should that be "Hattie Hotwheels—Superheroine"?'

Matty groaned. 'No, please! What an idiotic thing to do!'

'You were magnificent.' He kissed her. There was another flash as the photographer filled his boots with the kind of pictures any paparazzo would kill for. 'Marry me.'

'You need to think before you ask a girl something like that when she's had a shock,' she said, a little shakily. 'She might just say yes.'

'Give me your hand.' She lifted her right hand. 'No, the other one.' He took it, held it for a moment, then, ignoring the fact that they were surrounded by first-aiders, the boy's parents and half the people who'd come to the fête, he produced a ring from his pocket and said, 'I've thought about it. Wear this for me while you think about your answer.'

The stone was an emerald-cut yellow diamond, flanked by white brilliant diamonds. She looked up at him. 'Sebastian, it's beautiful.'

'Not as beautiful as you.'

And someone—it might just have been the photographer—shouted, 'Go on, lady, give him a kiss.'

'I'm no lady,' she murmured, as she gave him the kind

of kiss which answered any question he cared to ask. 'Which reminds me. I really should be getting out of these wet clothes...'

It was Sunday morning before Matty remembered why Sebastian should not have been in Sussex the day before.

Sebastian had made tea and a pile of toast, and brought it back to bed with the papers. They'd made the front page of at least two of them. 'What were you doing at the fête anyway?' she asked, tossing the papers on the floor. 'You were supposed to be at a meeting with some people interested in buying Coronet. Didn't they show?'

'I cancelled. I suddenly realised that the company isn't really mine to sell.'

That shouldn't have made sense, Matty thought, but she clearly knew him a lot better than she'd realised, because it did. Perfect sense. Coronet belonged to Blanche and all those other people who'd worked there for ever.

'So what happens now?'

'I'm going to organise a staff buy-out. Everyone can buy a penny share for every year they've worked for the company, which gives Blanche control. She's blossomed in the last couple of weeks, don't you think?'

'You seem to have that effect on women.' Unlike George, who had only ever seemed to think of himself. 'How did you find out you were George's son?'

Sebastian looked at her, clearly wondering at the leap between one statement and the next, but he let it go.

'Louise told me. She didn't mean to. I'd been sent home from school because there was an outbreak of mumps, which I thought was stupid, and Bea said, no, it was much worse for men because it made them really, really bad-tempered. Louise just laughed at her and told her not to be such a kid. Well, Bea wasn't having that.

She'd given Dad mumps before she went away to school, she said, and he was absolutely beastly. And Louise said not to be silly, if Dad had had mumps they wouldn't have been lumbered with a brat of a brother—at which point they both suddenly discovered they had something important to do.'

'I hadn't a clue what they were talking about, but when I got older it all made sense. Why my mother used to leave me at the office with George when she went up to town to go shopping. Why he took such an interest in me. Why he left me to sort out the company.'

'He got that right, at least.'

'You think he'd approve?'

'Actually, I don't think he ever considered anyone but himself. But I approve, if that counts for anything.'

'It counts for everything,' he said, abandoning his toast and hooking his arm over her head to hold her close. 'You are my whole world. Nothing and no one else matters. There's a way to go, but I'll keep a watching brief as advisor while they need me. And they've got you as consultant. They'll be fine.'

'You are fine.'

'Fine enough for you to give me an answer to the big question?'

She looked at the ring, then at him. 'How long can you wait?'

'As long as it takes. How long will it take?'

'Until Christmas. Ask me then, in the church next to the Hall. Ask me with your parents and your sisters and their husbands and kids and Guy and Fran sitting in those ancient pews. Ask me if I'll take you to be my lawful wedded husband there, with everyone we know and love as witnesses. I'll give you my answer then, Sebastian.'

'Is that the deal?'

'That's the deal,' she said.

'And in the meantime?'

'In the meantime, Mr Bigshot, we go to New York.'

It didn't snow, but everything was white with frost. Bright, clear, sparkling. The church bells were ringing a full peal; the choristers' voices sang of new hope, a new start.

Matty's chair took her to the door of the church, but in the porch she eased herself forward, took the crutches from Fran and levered herself to her feet. She'd been practising this for weeks, when Sebastian was in the office. She'd practised last night alone with Fran in the church. If Sebastian had guessed, he'd said nothing.

For him, but even more for herself, on this special day she was going to be, do, all that she was capable of.

Fran straightened the heavy cream velvet gown that fell from her shoulders, covering the braces on her legs.

Her hair... She'd thought of extensions, of having it long for today, but she wasn't that girl any more. Instead she'd kept the feathery cap, but it was streaked with purple and pink and gold for the occasion.

'Ready?' Fran asked at her side, her best friend, supporter.

'Ready,' she said.

She nodded to the verger, who gave a signal to someone out of sight. And the music started. Slow, stately, triumphant, step by step, using her hips to throw each leg in turn forward, shifting her weight from one leg to the other, pausing for balance, moving on. It might have been the slowest wedding march in history, but Sebastian was the most patient of grooms. His smile encouraged her every step of the way and her reward was to stand on her own two feet and look him in the face as she vowed to love and cherish him for the rest of her life.

**He's proud, passionate, primal—dare
she surrender to the sheikh?**

Feel warm winds blowing through your hair
and the hot desert sun on your skin as you are transported
to exotic lands…. As the temperature rises, let yourself be
seduced by our sexy, irresistible sheikhs.

In ***Traded to the Sheikh*** by Emma Darcy,
Emily Ross is the prisoner of Sheikh Zageo bin
Sultan al Farrahn—he seems to think she'll
trade her body for her freedom! Emily must
prove her innocence before time runs out….

TRADED TO THE SHEIKH

on sale April 2006.